AN UNSEEN ATTACKER...

Kent grabbed his bottle.

"M'lord," the blind man pleaded. "Didn't I say—"

"That you didn't see anyone," he finished.

"Exactly."

"Well, then?"

"But that's who hit you!"

After a heroic effort that almost choked him, Kent managed to focus on the blind man's nose, which damn near crossed his eyes. "Zero, this is not working."

Zuller leaned closer, beckoned with a manicured finger, and, when Kent rallied the muscle group that permitted him to lower his head, whispered, "He was invisible."

"The hell you say."

DON'T MISS BOOK ONE OF THIS HIGHLY UNLIKELY SERIES:
Kent Montana and the Really Ugly Thing from Mars

KENT MONTANA AND THE REASONABLY INVISIBLE MAN

LIONEL FENN

ACE BOOKS, NEW YORK

It's not what you see that will hurt you, but what you don't see that will curdle your shorts and keep the cat on the front porch;

And it's not what you don't see that will hurt you, but what you wish you could see that will probably zap you in the prime of life and make you wish you'd had your eyes checked;

And if any of this makes sense, then so will this stupid book.

—Timothy Boggs
(famous unpublished author)

– I –

The Homecoming

◆ 1 ◆

It was foggy that night.

In Merkleton.

England.

And the autumn moon rose above the surrounding low hills, barely piercing the night, while owls in the woodland called, and foxes in the fields answered.

The streets and alleys glittered and gleamed from the afternoon's rain.

Pedestrians hurried along the wide pavements with heads bowed and shoulders hunched, turning away from the occasional chilled breeze that rose with the fog from the dark waters of the River George.

Still, there was a definite festive air about the village this dark, damp, late September evening. Cheerful banners hung across the main road, many cottages and most of the shops had gaily painted posters well placed in their windows, hundreds of colored lights had been strung here and there on bush and tree, and fresh royal bunting had been affixed to the tall and spiraled iron fencing that marked the High Street boundary of the village's small park.

The four hotels were filled, bed-and-breakfast establishments had no more beds, and most of the pubs had no room at the inn.

It was the weekend of the Red Moon Festival, and the tourists were welcomed heartily, like eager fat sheep at a lean wolf's den.

Yet the regular patrons of the King's Hump, in Rains Lane, paid scant attention to the man who walked through the door just after nine o'clock. He was rather tall for a Merkleton stranger, reasonably well dressed save for the ugly yellow Barrymore hat whose floppy brim covered most of his face, and currently engaged in swiping tenacious puffs of fog from his not inconsiderable shoulders.

As he made his way toward the back, he spoke to no one and acknowledged no grunted greeting, soon finding himself a fairly comfortable position beside a squared post where the dark oak bar made an unannounced right turn into the paneled wall. Curiously enough, it was the only area of the room where the light did not extend sufficiently to reveal the features beneath his hat.

Curiously enough, he didn't take the hat off.

But once established, he reached into his trouser pocket to pull out a handful of coins, studied them for several seconds, then deftly dropped several onto the counter and ordered a pint of bitter from the barmaid.

She looked at the money, squinted at him standing there in shadow, looked back at the money, and said pleasantly, "You haven't been here for a while, have you, sir? In the country, I mean to say."

What she could see of his answering smile was devastatingly rueful, and oddly familiar.

"Alas, no," he admitted with a slight trace of an accent.

"I'll need another twenty pence."

"You're kidding."

She half closed one eye and cocked a hip. "I only kid, sir, when I'm kidding. Which isn't very often."

Another coin fell to the wood surface. "Out of practice," he apologized mournfully.

Her water-reddened right hand scooped up the money while, at the same time, her left hand expertly snatched a large glass from the overhead rack. Before the coins had clattered into the till, that same right hand had taken hold of the ivory pump handle which, within seconds, had filled the glass with the refreshment he required.

He nodded.

She returned the nod and moved away to take another order while pinching the barman's rump to stop him from flirting with the night's supply of women, loose and otherwise.

The stranger passed the glass under his nose, then drank deeply, his eyes closed in private delight. A delicate touch of a finger to his upper lip to check for errant foam, and he ordered another, lifted the glass, and shifted inconspicuously until he could lean against the wall beside a closed and unmarked door and was able to take in most of the interior without moving his head.

No one met the gaze of his unseen eyes.

That was, for the time being, just fine with him.

He had traveled many thousands of miles to reach this very place, one of his favorite haunts in all the country, and he was quite content, for the moment, to remain unrecognized and unapproached.

Besides, if he weren't here, unrecognized, he'd be back in the Hotel Bowlingham on the High Street, where the only person who bothered to talk to him was the reflection in his mirror. Not that it was a bad hotel—he used it every time he stayed in this rustic corner of Britannia—but his top-floor room was barely large enough for the double bed, the narrow desk with attached blow dryer, and the even narrower wardrobe with attached color television; the lobby, while of a good size and well appointed with many upholstered armchairs and couches, held too many people too inclined to talk to people they didn't know; and the residents' bar was crowded tonight, noisy with rock music and eager young travelers, and too damn bright for his current introspective mood.

Thus, for solace and peace, the King's Hump.

He sipped.

He settled.

He was pleased that nothing seemed to have changed since his last visit:

The pub was neither spectacular nor quaint nor even vaguely historical. It was, in fact, the usual earthy establishment of its kind—lots of old polished wood, a providently long bar, padded bench seats lining the wainscoted walls, and a dozen or so small tables at which three people could sit comfortably if they were careful where they put their knees. Upstairs, like many of its country cousins, it also provided a quartet of individual small rooms, two with private bath, for casual travelers and those too blasted to get home without harm.

A surly young man and his tittering girlfriend stood at a fruit machine and attempted to beat the diabolical cousin to a one-armed bandit gambling device—mostly, the stranger noted, by the liberal use of obscene incantations, since feeding it money the usual way didn't appear to be working.

At the entrance, a stout blind man with a white accordion played a medley of Stephen Foster tunes.

By the descending stairway to the Gents, three women sat at a table and tried on each other's makeup amid several explosions of giggles and delighted snorts.

There was smoke and laughter in the air, an atmosphere of such conviviality that the stranger nearly burst into tears—not because he was still unrecognized, but because this very place held such dear and fond memories for him that he was very nearly overwhelmed.

It certainly beat staying in London, where, no doubt, he would have spent most of his time dodging the bloodthirsty Highland assassins his mother usually sent down from the family estate and winery on an unnamed Hebrides isle whenever she learned that he was in town.

He sighed, sipped, and eavesdropped as the barmaid tried to bribe the barman into pouring honey over the blind man's musical instrument.

Nothing had changed.

Even Mary Shweet, the wretchedly poor flower girl in the dank lane outside, still sang softly in the fog, trying to sell her pitiful collection of blossoms to those most inclined to charity and conscience.

No; all was as he remembered, and for that, he was eternally grateful. Occasional tranquillity was good for the soul.

The barmaid wiped the counter at his elbow and asked if he wanted another.

He looked doubtfully over his shoulder at the empty glass. "Actually I don't think so. I've not had much to eat today."

She was still, he noted, a rather healthy young woman for her profession, close to his own age, with more dark hair than she had head to grow it on, a pert upturned nose, and cheeks gently flushed from her job's nocturnal exertions. As he smiled, she wiped a hand over the hip of her snug but appropriate jeans. The blouse she wore, of the elasticized and embroidered peasant variety, had somehow managed to slip down off one gleaming shoulder. "Perhaps a half this time?"

He shook his head. "I'll wait a bit, if you don't mind."

"Doesn't bother me, mate," she replied offhandedly. A careless swipe at the counter with her cloth. The shoulder vanished. "Deric, damnit," she yelled then to the man at the fruit machine, "don't whack it so bloody hard! You've already done in three this month!"

Deric Sumland, a husky lad with a shock of red hair that matched his straggly mustache, shrugged, snickered, and gave a nudge to his half-drunk companion, Dora Feathers, a blonde of such sluttish proportions as to give many a married man the whimpers on a cold winter's night.

"Fool," she muttered.

"They always are, at that age."

She leaned against the bar to continue the conversation, but when the stranger withdrew deeper into the shadows, she straightened with a frown and said, "Order or not, pal, but don't take up my valuable space breathing when you could be drinking."

He laughed softly. "The landlady, I take it?"

A mock curtsy and "Flora Tatterall at your service" was her reply.

"In that case, a half."

And with fresh drink in hand, he examined the room yet another time and wondered what in hell he was going to do tomorrow. Which was precisely what he had been wondering since his arrival in country, three days earlier. Though he wasn't concerned about his financial situation, he had thus far been unable to contact his theatrical agent in order to ascertain what sorts of jobs were available to him on this side of the ocean.

His last viable employment, on the stateside continuing daytime drama *Passions and Power,* had ended with his forced removal from his long-standing role as an English butler—for trivial causes, most of which had to do with his gentle insistence on certain lines being rewritten for clarity, conviction, and dramatic impact. For some reason, the director seemed not to think that a butler, even one portrayed by a genuine Scottish baron, could have motives and motivation for serving afternoon tea and announcing the arrival of the bad guys.

It had been a classic clash of personalities.

And he was the one who'd come away thoroughly dented.

He looked at his glass. Somehow it had become empty.

The accordionist adroitly switched to waltz-time Simon and Garfunkel.

"Here for the big do?" the landlady asked, both her shoulders and her libido bare.

He frowned.

She pointed over her shoulder to a poster tacked to one of the posts. It listed the events of the Red Moon Festival, whose climax would take place at the famed Merkleton Ringstones, an archaeological bounty miraculously discovered in an oak grove by the river shortly after the Second World War. The closing ceremony promised to be an occasion of high drama, with a (one would hope) fictionalized sacrifice, and parties all over the place once the show was over and the visiting Druids had packed their robes and left town.

Keeping a smile to himself, he shook his head.

"Then how about another?"

"No," he decided. "A whiskey instead."

One well-plucked black eyebrow lifted in mild surprise. She had obviously not pegged him for a heavy drinker. "What shall it be, then?"

"Glenbannock, I think," he replied automatically, and realized too late that he had spoken too loudly, smack in the middle of one of the evening's natural conversational lulls.

The landlady stared.

The accordion player hit a dazzling series of sour notes.

The three women gasped.

Deric and Dora turned from the fruit machine and lifted their leather collars to hide their faces.

The silence was such that a dripping faucet sounded like a funeral cannon.

The man sighed.

The landlady nibbled on her lips and said, "Did you say . . . Glenbannock?"

He considered denying it.

Then she mouthed his name as a question.

"Oh hell," he snapped in mild disgust, swept off his hat, and brushed back his embarrassingly abundant ginger hair with one unhappy hand. "Yes, damnit, Flora. And you might as well make it a double."

Flora Tatterall slapped one hand to her chest and gasped in delighted recognition.

Deric drew a knife from beneath his leather coat and slipped it into his pocket.

And the accordionist cried out in delight, "Well, I'll be a monkey's, lads, it's his lordship, Kent Montana!"

There was nothing Kent could say, and so he said nothing because, at that very moment, the lights went out, somebody screamed, there was a faint twanglike humming in his ear, and someone laid what felt like a steel pipe across the back of his head.

How frequently must one drink if one is to permanently damage one's liver? pondered Lizzy Howgath as she considered the evening's first brimming pint of lager now set before her on the tiny scarred table. It seemed to her that six a night for several decades ought to do it right enough, though she was reluctant to trust the test results of the most recent National Health survey. She was also reluctant to acknowledge the blandishments of the gentleman leaning against the bar directly opposite her, though his large brown eyes had been keenly observing her since the moment she'd wandered in, plopped herself down, and commenced her experiment.

Not that she wasn't affected by his attention.

He was, after all, a rather decent-looking young man in a snug wool roll-top sweater, a rakish tweed cap, and high polished boots that reflected the pub's lights like slightly smeared stars. He also made no attempt to join her, clearly and politely awaiting an invitation.

Should she or shouldn't she?

She drank.

She followed the progress of a taller, more aristocratic type who wasted no time digging himself into the bar's far corner without so much as a glance in her direction.

Now, that one she might be interested in, she admitted without an ounce of shame. His bearing, his manner, his attitude, his demeanor, all synonymous with class and wealth.

Except for that stupid hat.

She cupped the glass between her palms.

With luck, he might even be the one she had been searching for all this time, the one she could talk to, could share her burdens with, to whom she could reveal the guilty secret that festered within her even now, causing her to belch in a most unladylike manner, causing her aerobically flat stomach to flutter, causing her violet eyes to water whenever she recalled the horrible consequences of her continued silence.

Yes, it might well be he, but would he listen?

Would he believe her?   •

Would anyone in this place believe her if they knew the

terror which, at this very moment, might be stalking them as if they were the prey of some diabolical hunt?

Sadly she doubted it.

Instead they would laugh; they would call her a common drunkard; they would tease her until the tears flowed; then, in fits and starts of hypocritical remorse, they would ply her with more drink in order to smooth the rough edges of their social consciences.

But they would not believe her.

She trapped a self-pitying sob before it escaped, swallowed it, and followed it with a long draught of lager. A dainty handkerchief to cleanse her full, dark lips. A trembling hand to smooth a fall of silken black hair away from her left eye. A determined lift of her proud chin when the brown-eyed gentleman cleared his throat and crossed the narrow space between them.

"Pardon me, miss," he said respectfully, pulling off his cap and fair crushing it to his chest, "but as you're alone, and I am as well, would it be an imposition if I sat with you for a while?" He raised his hand quickly. "Just for a talk, that's all. I've no other intentions."

Lizzy considered the smooth lines of his young face, surely a good decade younger than she, and finally, almost fearfully, nodded.

He smiled and found a spare, backless chair, drew it opposite her, and sat gingerly, as if ready to bolt for the exit at a single harsh word from her.

"Stan," he said, holding out a bold hand. "Stan Yarkshore."

She accepted the hand, found the grip refreshingly steady and dry, and shyly gave him her own name.

He nodded.

She sipped.

"Well, Miss Howgath," he said, smiling so broadly his pudgy cheeks dimpled, "what brings you here? I'm a regular myself, and I don't recall seeing you before."

Should I tell him? she wondered. Dare I speak the words that cry to be free?

"A long day's spending my money, I'm afraid," she answered, not quite a lie and not quite the entire truth. She pointed to a bulging shopping bag nestled beside her on the floor. "I've been so terribly bad that I even missed my train connection."

"Ah," he said, leaning back. "I thought you wasn't from around here. Kent, is it?"

Pleased, she grinned, and lied again. "Liverpool, actually."

"Ah, a song there to be sung, I wouldn't doubt," he said solemnly.

She chuckled at his wit.

He chuckled with her and begged her to permit him to bring the next round.

"Oh, I couldn't, Stan, not really."

A wink, and a finger to the side of his nose. "Not a poor thing like that," he said, pointing to the dregs of her lager. "I was suggesting something more elegant, if you don't mind my saying so. A liqueur, perhaps? To keep us in the Festival spirit?"

He will get me drunk, and I will spill all, she feared.

"If you wish," she said coyly.

He clapped his hands once. "Splendid! Allow me."

And he was gone, easing his way through the crush at the bar, leaving her to wonder what in the name of heaven had possessed her. This was dangerous. She might grow to like him. Lord, she might even grow affectionate. And what would happen then? Would it be like all the others? Would he find himself in the gutter in the morning, his face all a mess, his clothes torn and bloodied, his legs smashed, his arms useless, his eyes black and blue?

She panted.

She sniffed.

Good heavens, Lizzy, she cautioned, you're getting all excited.

But it was too late to flee. The three harridans sitting near the door were eyeing her jealously, and the portly blind accordionist had evidently sensed her emotional confusion and had swung smoothly into a soothing medley of tunes derived from stage shows featuring animals ranging from alley cats to armadillos.

Her right hand then drifted down to the bag, holding it closed, hefting it once to be reassured of its weight. For there were no gifts or condiments hidden therein beneath the pink tissue paper she'd stolen from a tony newsagent on the High Street. No, not at all.

What was there was her life, and more.

"How's this, then?"

She jumped, almost screamed, when Stan settled again into his chair and placed a glass before her.

He frowned at her distress. "Are you all right?"

Her throat abruptly dry, she nonetheless managed a nod. "Woolgathering," she confessed. "I'm sorry."

"Nothing to be sorry about, love," he replied. He lifted his brandy and toasted her. "Cheers, to a beautiful woman."

She picked up her own glass, eyes properly downcast, and murmured thanks for the compliment. Sipped. Coughed at the strong liquid. And outrageously permitted him to wipe the resultant tear from her cheek with a gentle, soft finger.

The barmaid yelled something at the couple messing about with the fruit machine.

He leaned forward then, cap shoved back on his head. "I think we've a possible friendship growing here, Lizzy, if I may be so bold."

Her heart leapt up when she beheld the rainbow reflected on the skin of his scalp. Normally such lack of hair on a man repelled her, but this pate was different. It issued warmth, it commanded respect, it was bold and required no apologies for its loss. She wanted to rub it. She wanted to kiss it. She wanted to feel it against her breast before it was split irreparably in twain and ran red with gushing blood.

Oh lord, what's come over you, girl?

Stan winked at her, slow and steady.

"Mr. Yarkshore," she said, easing him away with her palm, "I do think you're a bit forward, don't you?"

His smile was apologetic. "Perhaps it's the drink."

"Perhaps."

"And perhaps it's the sun that shines so brightly from those cheeks."

She blushed.

He winked.

Flustered, seeking something to talk about and sensing he wasn't the type to care much about politics or religion, she spied the stranger. "Do you know who that is?"

He looked quickly, looked back. "Nope. Never seen him before. A friend of yours?"

"Oh no, I don't know him," she protested. "But you said you were . . . that is, you indicated that you came in here often, and I just wondered . . . I mean, it's possible you don't know, whereas I, a perfect stranger myself, would have never seen him before in my life. You see?''

"My dear, dear Lizzy," he said, reaching across the table to cover her free hand.

Leave, she ordered; my god, girl, leave now, before it's too late!

"Stan," she said, leaning forward herself, "I have a story to tell you."

He nodded wisely. "I thought as much."

"You did?"

"Lizzy, I'm a simple man, but I'm not so simple as not to recognize a soul in anguish, especially when it sits so prettily across from me." He patted her hand. "We probably won't see each other again, you and I, so what better man to unburden yourself to?"

She considered; she frowned; she squinted when her vision went blurry quite suddenly and she thought she saw a metal pipe drift behind Stan's head. She blinked furiously. The illusion vanished.

"Stan," she said urgently, "promise you will not laugh?"

"Laugh? At you? Not bloody likely, if you'll excuse the language."

"And promise you won't interrupt until I'm done?"

"If you want."

"I want."

"Then," he said with a wave of his hand, "your wish is my command."

She emptied her glass.

She emptied his glass.

She picked up the bag and held it close to her chest.

"You see," she said, "it all began when—"

The lights went out.

And somebody screamed.

Lurking was not something Angus Dean did well. Whenever he was required to fill out a form listing his skills and education, lurking was always placed at the bottom of the list. He hated it. Sneaking about, ducking into doorways, pretending to study window displays, pretending to read newspapers, crossing the street when he really didn't want to—it was all rubbish as far as he was concerned. Rot. And fairly on the cowardly side to boot.

He preferred the direct approach, the result of his twenty-three years in the British Army, mustered out only five years ago and cast upon the doleful sea to fend for himself. Not for him the whisper when a damned good shout would do. Not for him to hide behind the skirts of a trench coat and secret code words when his green velvet jacket would suit the occasion just as neatly.

You learned things when you were in the army.

You learned to keep your hair short in case you had to leave your bed in a hurry; you learned to keep your back straight so your six feet and sixteen stone showed themselves to best advantage; you learned to glare as only a Royal Sergeant Major can, thus reducing the opposition to a quivering mass of pudding you could poke and prod to your heart's content.

That's what you learned in the army.

None of this damned lurking.

On the other hand, the money was good, the hours weren't so bad, and as long as it didn't require him to think for very long, he supposed he could manage it.

Especially since he was being paid by two different people to do the same thing, even though the two different people didn't know the other one was paying too.

At the moment he lurked across the street from the King's Hump, leaning casually against the brick wall that formed the Lane's northern boundary. He felt like a fool. All those idiots in there, drinking and laughing the night away, and here he was, out in the street, so to speak, hands jammed into the pockets of his dark blue peacoat, head covered by a wool seaman's cap, nose turning red from the nip in the air, and all because his instructions were to keep an eye on the lady in the red coat, and not, if he could help it, let her leave town without learning her destination.

Now how was he supposed to do that by standing out here?

Rains Lane itself was quite narrow, little more than an alley, really, that opened onto the High Street on the one end and a paved-over park at the other. The only light came from the pub windows and a yellow globe over a restaurant called Wagner's, both on the other side. Otherwise, there was nothing but stone or brick walls, damp now with the kind of fog he hadn't seen since he was a lad, prowling the streets of London for a bit of excitement and the occasional theatrical experience.

It had begun as a mist not seen at all, felt only on his face

and the backs of his hands; then wisps and snakes of it had
thickened and slipped across the already treacherous cobbles,
curled up the stone and brick facades of the buildings that
formed the alley, and he figured that, in an hour, it would
completely obliterate all sight and sound.

He stamped his feet to keep them warm and wished for a
cigar.

His head cocked when a sudden burst of laughter broke from
the open door of the pub.

He wondered if his cover would be blown if he walked over
to that accordionist and shoved that caterwauling mother-of-
pearl instrument down his bleedin' throat. Christ, he hated
accordions! They were worse than bagpipes, for god's sake,
and vaguely obscene what with all that pushing and pulling
and puffing and bellowing. Maybe the guy would do him a
favor and drop dead.

He snarled.

On the other hand, maybe he would find that damned flower
girl, buy all her wares, and send her home. Her voice, so
tremulous and sweet, made his stomach churn. He wondered
if she was related to the accordion player.

He snarled again.

He flattened himself harder against the wall when approaching footsteps echoed softly off the ground. A squint, a held
breath, but he could see nothing, no one, and he chanced a
step forward in order to ascertain the walker's direction.

No one was there.

He was alone.

That didn't surprise him. Fog did that to a man—tricked his
senses into believing things were what they seemed when they
weren't that way at all if the man had any sense. Even now,
the traffic on the High Street sounded a million miles away
instead of only thirty yards, and the winos singing in the park,
a like distance to his right, could have been in France for all
their words were understood.

Aye, the fog was like that.

No friend at all to man or beast.

The fog thickened; the light dimmed.

He pulled out his hands and rubbed them briskly, sidled
away from his hiding place, and peered through the smoke and
bodies to make sure the woman in red was still there.

She was.

Sitting at one of those stupid wee tables, talking to a guy easily half her age.

Angus grinned without mirth.

Too bad the fool didn't know what he was in for, trying to chat her up, get her drunk, probably hoping to lure her back to his squalid little flat where he could do any number of disgusting things Angus himself had learned during his frequent tours of duty in Germany and the Near East. Too bad. The guy hadn't a prayer.

His laugh was more a grunt.

It would serve the poor dope right if he quit his lurking, walked in, and exposed her right then and there. It would be good for a laugh, that's for sure, though he doubted his employer, either one of them, would see the full ramifications of the humor.

He caught a sneeze on his sleeve.

His hands found their pockets.

The glazed windows of the pub grew increasingly translucent, and he figured that if this were daylight, the fog would have prevented him from seeing anything at all. He didn't like it. It was bad enough, all this lurking about and pretending to be a sailor separated from his ship in case he was asked what the hell he was doing, lurking about Rains Lane; now, if he wanted to keep an eye on the lady, he'd have to leave his current position and move closer.

One eye closed in contemplation.

In point of fact, that wouldn't be such a bad idea. He could nip inside for a pint, then take it outside and stand against the wall. All perfectly legitimate. And it would allow him to look in now and then, as if hoping for a free space along the walls or at a table.

He nodded.

Lurking without looking like he was lurking.

Angus, he thought, you haven't lost the touch, by god, you haven't.

He stepped onto the cobbles, one hand free, the other fumbling for some money.

Then someone cried a name, the lights went out, and someone inside let out a scream.

"Has it occurred to you," said Hazel Bloodlowe as she adjusted her imitation fox fur coat more snugly around her throat and fluffed her tower of brunette curls, "that we could be home right now—respectively speaking, of course—watching that aphid-and-rose special on BBC 1, or Benny Hill on 2, instead of standing around here like a couple of hookers?"

"Yes, it has occurred to me," Janice Plase answered glumly. Her feet ached. She hated wearing high heels, hated black mesh stockings, hated the tartan miniskirt so snug around her bottom that it felt as if she were wearing one of her mother's corsets. She was also jealous of Hazel, who got to wear the three-quarter-length fox fur with the ermine trim while all she had to protect her from the weather was a thin lamb's wool coat that made her look as if she were waiting for a convenient funeral to come along. "But I am also reminded that we are supposed to be hookers."

With a disgusted snort Hazel excavated a compact from her handbag, snapped it open, and checked her cherry-bright lipstick, her cobalt eye shadow, and what looked like nine-foot eyelashes. "It's demeaning."

"It's our job."

"Well, believe me, job or not, I am going to complain to Easewater first thing in the morning, if I live that long. God, where the hell did this damn fog come from? And why the hell do *we* have to do this?"

"Because we're women, I suppose."

"Besides that."

"I don't know. Because we look like hookers?"

"Besides that."

"For heaven's sake, Hazel, what the hell do you want from me?"

"I don't know. I reckon I'm just tired."

All evening long they had been patiently pacing a tottering trail along the High Street from the elegant Hotel Druid down there opposite the village park, to the Hotel Bowlingham. Nearly two hundred dismal yards and a couple of blocks of loose paving stones, leering tourists, drunken Druids, and a snorting German shepherd rooting through the plastic trash bags. Most of the shops that marked the street's commerce had long since closed for the day, and none of the hotels they passed looked even remotely inviting. Not to mention the occasional whiff of the River George at low tide, whose mud flats were famous for their curative powers. Yet they were required to ply their bogus trade until, they had been informed at their afternoon briefing, they were able to make positive contact with person or persons unknown who would, in the course of things and if nobody screwed up, lead them to a delicious series of reasonably legal entrapments which would, God and Her Majesty willing, up their arrest rate impressively.

"Tired," Hazel repeated in a dull monotone, peering into Rains Lane where, the briefing had also suggested, their man, or men, was, or were, likely to be. In a pub. Where they ought to be right now if they were going to do this damn thing right, and the hell with regulations. "Lord and damn, I am just so tired I could lie down and die."

"Of course you're tired," Janice agreed sympathetically. "But so am I. So is half of bloody England. But we have a job to do, Hazel. And because we are who we are, and because no one else can do this miserable assignment, or was daft enough to volunteer, we have to make sure we don't go balls up on it, okay? If we blow it, if we don't get this mystery person or persons unknown, there'll be hell to pay with Inspector Easewater, and you and I will be handing out tickets to sods who can't read parking signs."

"Thank you, Miss Plase."

"No sweat, Miss Bloodlowe."

"Jesus, we sound like a music hall act."

"I wouldn't know. I'm not old enough to remember music halls."

"Neither am I. Was my mum told me all about it."

Janice grinned.

Hazel sighed.

Janice tugged at her skirt again and told herself not to get so discouraged, that this was all part of the job and she really had no right to complain. After all, no one had forced her into a career of fighting crime, no one had held a gun to her head and threatened the decimation of her IQ if she didn't put on the uniform. It had been her own decision. Preserving the law, apprehending felons and politicians, and sweeping the streets clear of all that was anathema to her sense of what was right.

Hazel, in one of her more bitchy moments, had suggested that Janice had signed up because she couldn't get a man, couldn't hold a job, and couldn't stand living at home, in Canterbury, with her parents, who, until Janice turned thirteen, had dressed and treated her like a boy because, before she was born, they had prayed at the cathedral every Christmas for a

male child and refused to believe God had been so peckish as
to deny their wish.

Hazel couldn't have been more wrong.

Canterbury was beautiful this time of year.

Besides, some of the clothes weren't all that bad. At least
the sweaters were much nicer than what the other girls wore.
The shoes were a bitch, though.

Her partner glanced forlornly along the street. "I am not
going to make that hike again."

"Well, maybe we ought to go down there again, just in
case," Janice suggested, intently peering through her glitter-
coated veil into the shadowed, fog-filled alley that was Rains
Lane. They had already passed through it twice, nearly toppling
off their heels because of the cobblestones. Hazel, however,
had vetoed stopping at the King's Hump both times; she didn't
want to make themselves any more obvious than they already
were. "That sailor could give us extra cover, if you know what
I mean."

"Extra cover?" Hazel peered at her with one eye closed.
"Janice, do you have any idea why we're out here?"

"Of course! To make contact with a mystery man. Or men."

"And then what?"

Janice blinked. "Well . . ."

"Oh god," Hazel said quietly.

Janice grinned. "I know, I know—you're tired. So let's just
go to the sailor—"

"I told you before, I don't want to talk to any drunken
sailor."

"He's not drunk, silly. He's just standing there, for heaven's
sake. I'll bet he's broke. Probably waiting for someone to come
out of Wagner's so he can hit them up for the price of a drink."

"Wagner's is closed."

Janice frowned. "It is?"

"It closed an hour ago."

"It did?"

"Of course it did. Locked up right after those guys walked
past us."

"What guys?"

"Oh god, Janice, didn't you see them?"

"No, of course not."

"Great hooker you'd make."

"Oh yeah. And what did they look like, then?"

"Well, how should I know? I was watching the pub, wasn't I, just like I'm supposed to. All I know is, the first one, he had this really stupid hat on. Looked like Garbo in drag. Didn't give me a notice, the jerk."

"He wore a dress?"

"Janice, for god's sake."

"Okay, okay. What about the second one?"

"I don't know. I didn't see him at all."

"What? We're standing right here, a guy has to trip over us to get into the Lane, and you didn't see him?"

"I was looking at the night porter taking the air down there, the one from the Bowlingham. He's cute."

"So how did—"

"I heard him. I have very good ears. Makes it very hard, sleeping at night. But I heard him."

Janice scowled. "I didn't."

"You probably didn't hear that scream, either," Hazel said, heading quickly into the Lane.

"What scream?"

·2·

Reflexes trained by years of dropping laden supper trays whenever the director yelled "Action," Kent grabbed the brass bar rail on his way down. Impressive whirling stars accompanied him; stars not nearly so bright, however, as his outrage at being ambushed, the result of which was a severe emotional turmoil which prevented him from blacking out completely—along with a little help from the thickness of his hair and the fact that the pipe had merely sideswiped him, after all.

What an idiot! he thought angrily as he settled closer to the floor and waited for his vision to clear; as soon as I let down my guard, Mother strikes in the night. What a fool! What a blind, stupid fool!

The steel pipe struck again, this time rebounding off the rail not an inch from his thumb, striking sparks and terror into the vision and hearts of those trying to get out of harm's way and not doing a very good job of it since all the lights were still out.

He snatched his hand away, dropped all the way to the floor and, in a fit of agility, rolled hastily to his right. His head decided to remain in one piece, at least for the time being; but it was a hard job, what with all the shrieking going on, the footsteps racing madly here and there, and the pipe connecting solidly with the paneling at just about the height where his forehead would have been had he not moved.

He rolled again.

The persistent weapon struck too close for comfort, and he wondered as he backed against the wall if the assassin had some power that enabled him to see in the dark.

Quickly he pushed himself to his feet, peered through the

blackness, and felt rather than heard the pipe swing for another go. He shifted nimbly to his right and heard the simultaneous sound effect of Deric screaming in pain and the *smush* of the pipe landing solidly on the man's shoulder.

Someone shouted for the police.

An ungodly wail rose at the door.

Glass shattered.

Someone else was struck, and screamed accordingly.

Undeterred by all the commotion, the pipe descended once more, this time on the glass face of the fruit machine, which, in its own mechanical way, celebrated its demise by emitting a startling shower of sparks and flame that managed to redouble the screaming and the shouting and the running and the falling and the knocking over of tables and chairs. On the plus side, it did provide Kent with just enough light to recoil in horror at the scene before him:

tables and chairs knocked over;

people running this way and that, attempting to escape without leaping through the windows;

Deric prone on the floor and grabbing his left shoulder while Dora bellowed for medical evacuation;

a tall sailor plunging militarily into the room against the current;

two hookers wrestling with a man in a tweed cap, who seemed to be holding on to one of their handbags;

a woman in a truly foul red coat lashing out with her feet and shopping bag at anyone who came near her;

and the pipe.

At last unmanned, it lay at the base of the demolished gambling machine, dented, scarred, and smoking at one end.

The lights came on.

All the screaming and shouting and running and knocking and falling over stopped as if someone had pulled a plug.

With one hand gingerly massaging the back of his neck, Kent knelt by the offensive weapon and poked at it charily with a finger. When it didn't fly up and bash in his teeth, he reached into a hip pocket, pulled out a handkerchief, and very carefully picked it up.

He stood.

He made his way to the bar as if trodding on eggs and leaned against it, winced at a persistent needle boring tiny holes in his skull, and held his murderous burden close to a bulb that hung over the counter.

"What is it?" asked the landlady.

He looked up without raising his head. She had a shotgun in one hand, a gnarled club in the other, and both shoulders had bared themselves delightfully and inappropriately above her peasant blouse. Behind her, he could see several of the regulars already beginning to straighten the place up.

The hookers were gone.

The woman in red was gone.

The sailor was gone.

"It's a pipe," he answered judiciously, returning his attention to both woman and weapon.

"Are you all right?"

He didn't nod; that would have been suicidal. "I expect so."

She replaced the shotgun in its rack under the bar, the club in its sheath beside the till. "Who did it?"

"Don't know. The lights went out."

The blind man bellowed imaginative imprecations vis-à-vis the permanent damage done to his precious accordion.

"Aren't you going after him?"

"I take one step," he told her, "and I'm going to keel over." A quick glance at the fogbound door. "Besides, with any luck, he's long gone by now."

"It's them Druids, no doubt," she said in disgust. "Give them a robe, they want the whole sacrifice."

Deric moaned, rolled to a sitting position, and allowed Dora to assist him awkwardly to his feet. Together they staggered to a wall bench, where the redhead somewhat ill-naturedly accepted the ministrations of half a dozen makeshift medics.

"I don't like trouble in my place," Flora complained.

"Wasn't me that started it," Kent reminded her.

"I didn't say it was, your lordship. But it's funny, isn't it, how you, of all people, were picked up to be bashed."

The thought had occurred to him.

He had also concluded, albeit reluctantly, that this wasn't the handiwork of his mother, desperate though she may be to rid him of his ancestral title, sell all his land, and retire to Majorca to raise whatever the hell she could get her hands on out there. It was much too direct, much too *common*. Poisons and mad dogs, heat-seeking missiles and global catastrophe were more her style.

No, it had been someone else.

Someone who had arbitrarily determined that he should not leave this pub alive.

A madman. A psychomanic. An old flame. His old director on *Passions and Power*. A quick strike, in and out, and ultimately unsuccessful.

So who the hell was it?

Unless, reason suggested, he simply happened to be just one of three unlucky victims. An innocent bystander. A luckless recipient of fickle chance.

Flora leaned over the bar and tapped his shoulder, an indication that she wanted to check the condition of his skull. He obeyed, grimaced when she parted his hair, and held his breath with a hiss when her fingers danced smoothly and expertly over his scalp. That he was, at the same time, in a position to examine the marvelously intricate hand-stitching that kept her neckline from plunging like a skittish stock market to her waist was little consolation for the agony he suffered. Well . . . , he amended when she leaned even closer and hummed to herself, perhaps a bit more than a little, though he was too much of a gentleman to actually whistle or sigh.

The sigh came when she completed her examination.

"Just a small lump," she declared. "You were lucky."

"Oh aye, I could use more luck like that," he answered sourly.

The blind man drop-kicked his ruined accordion into the alley and demanded to know who the hell was going to pay for his abrupt loss of income.

Flora, a wary eye on those who had nearly completed the hasty cleanup, reached under the bar and thumped a fresh bottle of Glenbannock on the counter. Two glasses followed. A twist of the wrist had the cap off.

"Allow me," he said gallantly, and poured them each a generous portion.

"That'll be five quid," she said blandly. "In advance, if you please."

"What?"

"Five."

"But Flora, I have just been cruelly assaulted! A respected, if not terribly well known, peer of this hallowed realm has been bashed about the head and shoulders before your very

eyes! The least you can do is buy me one drink, for heaven's
sake.''

She lifted the glass from his hand. ''*I'll* buy you a beer.
You'll buy me one of these.'' She winked saucily. ''You're
the baron, remember? I'm just a simple merchant.''

He stared, nearly glared, then counted out the money.

She smiled and tipped a finger under her chin. ''Thank you,
sir.'' And gave him back his glass.

''Right.'' He drank. ''Right.'' He drank again.

The blind man unerringly stomped the length of the room,
demanding instant charitable contributions to his recently established replacement fund, bewailing his manifold woes and
the fact that he wouldn't be able to make a pitiful penny come
the Red Moon Festival, and finally stopped next to Kent to
prop his elbows heavily on the bar.

''Y'know,'' he said glumly, ''life's a high note, and then
you're a dead note.''

''Bugger off, Zero,'' Flora snarled.

''Me squeeze box is dead,'' he wailed.

''And I thank God for it,'' she snapped, rolled her eyes at
Kent, and retreated to the rest of her customers, who, after the
excitement, were ready to drink her dry.

Kent refilled his glass. ''Not to worry, Zero. You couldn't
play that thing anyway.''

Zero Zuller drew himself up and snorted. ''The hell you
say.''

''The hell I say.'' When Flora wasn't looking, he reached
under the counter and snatched another tumbler. A small one.
And filled it. ''Have a drink.''

The blind man smacked his lips. ''I do thank you, but what's
the catch?''

''If you don't drink it, I will.''

Zuller drank. Wiped his lips with a gold cashmere sleeve.
Took off his dark glasses and pinched the bridge of his red-
veined nose between thumb and forefinger. ''Can't see a damn
thing with them on,'' he complained.

''You're blind, stupid.''

''And don't I know it,'' Zuller retorted. ''But I ain't so blind
that I didn't see the guy what coshed you.''

Kent, already feeling the faintly pleasant multiple effects of
several swallows of his private stock of forty-year-old whiskey,
was unable to give the man the significant look his news de-

served. He had to content himself by merely blinking slowly, once, and saying, "Huh?"

"The guy what belted you. I saw him."

Kent sniffed, looked over at Flora, looked around the blind man at Deric enjoying the attention his injury brought him, looked at the smoking dead fruit machine, then looked at the blind man again. "Zero," he said carefully, "though I risk the wrath of our hostess, the inestimable Miss Tatterall, I will buy you the best accordion money can buy if you're telling me the truth."

Zuller touched a grateful finger to his lemon cashmere driving cap. "M'lord," he said, "that's a fine offer you're making."

"Don't go humble on me, you great idiot. I know you too well. Just tell me what the guy looked like."

"I don't know. I didn't see him."

"No kidding."

Zuller's cherubic-except-for-the-veins face took on a pained expression. He sniffled. His lips trembled. "Does that mean I don't get me accordion?"

The hookers returned to the pub and planted themselves rather disgruntledly just around the corner from Kent and the blind man. Though Eddie the barman straightened his bow tie and flattened his eyebrows, Flora only scowled at them. But she said nothing. Considering the damages suffered by the stampede, as long as they paid—as long as someone paid—for their drinks, she was prepared to be magnanimous.

Using all the skills acquired through years of acting in daytime dramas, Kent read all this in her expression, and he admired her for it. He also had no truck with the world's oldest profession; on the other hand, the blonde in the lamb's wool coat wasn't half bad on the old bloodshot eyes.

"No," he said. "You do not get the accordion."

"But your lordship—"

"Enough."

He poured them each another drink. Flora held up ten fingers. Zuller held up one. The hookers, red-faced and puffing as if they'd just run a mile, dropped their handbags solidly onto the counter and ordered double scotches.

Kent grabbed his bottle.

"M'lord," the blind man pleaded. "Didn't I say—"

"That you didn't see anyone," he finished.

"Exactly."

"Well, then?"

"But that's who hit you!"

After a heroic effort that almost choked him, Kent managed to focus on the blind man's nose, which damn near crossed his eyes. "Zero, this is not working."

Zuller leaned closer, beckoned with a manicured finger, and, when Kent rallied the muscle group that permitted him to lower his head, whispered, "He was invisible."

"The hell you say."

The blind man crossed himself and held up three fingers, frowned, changed it to two fingers, frowned and crossed himself again. "I swear."

A single deep breath later, Kent wondered just how drunk he was to be able to say, with a perfectly straight face, "How do you know he was invisible?"

Zuller's eyes shifted craftily side to side. "Because I couldn't see him, that's why."

Kent dropped a comforting hand on the man's shoulder. "Zero, you couldn't see him because you are blind."

One of the hookers sneezed.

The other one asked for a cup of tea.

Deric demanded compensation for the loss of his gambling shoulder.

"No," Zuller insisted. "I couldn't see him because he was invisible. Well, part of him was anyway."

Kent watched Flora deliver the tea, saw the blonde in the lamb's wool coat that really wanted a good cleaning pull something out of her handbag and show it to the landlady. Flora squinted at it, squinted at the blonde, and shrugged. The blonde smirked. The brunette sneezed.

"Zero," he said, "how can a man be only partly invisible?"

"Well, how the hell should I know? Begging your pardon, your lordship."

I am, Kent thought, trapped in a hallucinatory dream of my mother's manufacture. She's spiked the Glenbannock. She's pumped some kind of noxious gas into the room. Or . . . I am supremely drunk.

"Okay," he said, straightening and smiling at how clear the air was up there. "Which part was visible?"

"The pipe."

"Ah. The pipe."

"And a couple other bits too, I think. But I couldn't really tell. It was dark, you know."

"And you're blind."

"Well, there's that too."

Kent reached into his pocket and pulled out a twenty-pound note. After snapping it flat to prove its worth, he placed it squarely under the bottle of Glenbannock and whistled sharply until Flora looked in his direction. He pointed at the money, the bottle, and the blind man. Then he blew her a kiss, put the pipe in his topcoat pocket, adjusted that topcoat artfully about his shoulders, decided the hell with the hat, and headed for the door.

"Hey, wait a minute!" Zuller called after him.

He stopped.

"Ain't you gonna go after the guy that hit you?"

Kent's smile was infuriatingly benign. "I can't see him, Zero, I can't chase him."

The blind man appealed urgently to the room at large. "Then what about my accordion?"

"Put a sock in it, you daft idiot," Flora yelled.

Kent walked on.

"Hey! Damnit, your lordship, what the bloody hell about my goddamn new accordion?"

He paused at the threshold and looked out at the fog, felt the chill, felt the damp, and snapped his collar up. His hotel was only a few yards away, up to the end of the alley and a brisk left turn onto the High Street. Which, when he peered out, he couldn't see because of the fog, but he knew it was there.

And so, perhaps, was his assailant.

His head hurt.

The blind man was still screaming about his accordion.

Considering the alternative if he returned inside, and considering the pipe that weighed heavily in his pocket, and considering the known fact that one more drink would lay him flat on his back, he had no choice.

He stepped over the threshold.

Into a soundless grey world that swallowed him whole.

Janice Plase tugged as unobtrusively as she could at the hem of her tartan miniskirt, certain that every male eye in the room was determined to discover the color and texture of her knick-

ers. Every eye but one, that is—the eye, though either one
would have done, of the tall man at the bar the others kept
calling a lord. By the accent, she suspected he was from Scot-
land; by the slip of a tongue, that he was a baron; by the money
he laid on the counter, that he hadn't yet turned his estates into
a game park or swimming pool for the teeming unrelated
masses.

So what was a man like that doing in a place like this?

Hazel took off her coat.

Despite its condition, Janice declined to remove hers, because the blouse that went with the miniskirt was snug enough
to serve as sole support of her torso if she had half a mind and
the figure to go with it. As it was, she only accepted her scotch
and sipped at it gratefully, glad to be in out of the chill, even
for a few minutes.

This was a mess.

This was a disaster.

They were going to be sacked, no question about it.

No sooner had they responded to the scream and charged
into the pub, ready to announce themselves as police officers
and nab the man they don't know who it was, than some bald
fool had tried to snatch her purse under pretext of chasing a
frightened-looking woman in a godawful red coat. Janice had
slugged him, Hazel had shinned him, but it wasn't until someone had collided with their struggles that he'd broken loose
and escaped.

Then, just as they made to pursue the felon, Hazel had
yelped, whirled, and tried to slap the face of the man who had,
she explained testily afterward, made sharp advances upon her
rear. The trouble was, no one was there, and Janice suspected
that Hazel was beginning to feel the effects of too many days
on duty without a break, and too many nights in her flat without
benefit of something other than a cold shower.

Not that she approved of promiscuity and one-night stands,
but what the hell, as her mum used to say; whatever works,
and it beats looking like a prune.

"Hazel," she said, "why don't we call it a night?"

"Hush," her partner ordered, and pointed at the two men
conversing diagonally opposite them. One was the man she
had noticed right off, the other was the blind accordionist.

"What's up?"

"Hush!"

She shrugged. She sipped. She emptied her glass in a gulp and ordered a cup of tea.

Hazel sneezed and hushed herself.

Janice leaned her elbows casually on the bar, heard someone say "invisible," and looked askance at the man they called Kent Montana. He was a little under the weather, she guessed, from the way he kept staring at the blind man while rubbing the back of his neck, and she deduced, from the talk around her and the lump on the back of his head, that he was one of the two who had been attacked by someone wielding a steel pipe. The other was a largish redheaded lout moaning against the wall behind her.

Then she heard the word again, saw Montana rear back in clear disbelief, lean forward again, rear back, and stuff a bill under the bottle in front of him. When he bade the blind man a farewell and walked around her toward the exit, she swiveled cautiously, not wanting him to know he was under her watchful gaze.

And when he left without noticing her, she muttered, "Damn."

"What?" Hazel said impatiently.

"Nothing."

"Then don't swear on duty."

"Well, we're drinking on duty, aren't we?"

"That's different. That's called keeping our camouflage intact."

"We're hookers, remember?" she said.

"Hookers drink."

"Hookers swear."

"Hookers hook too, but we're not doing that, are we?"

Janice frowned. "What?"

"Don't start," Hazel warned. "Now, get after him before he goes away."

"After who?"

"Excuse me," interrupted the burly young redhead, easing manfully between them and turning his back solidly on Janice, "but don't I know you somewhere before?"

"No," Janice snarled.

"Could be," Hazel contradicted lightly, one hand fluttering to his stout arm, the other fluffing her curls. "And where would it be, then?"

"Hazel!" Janice hissed.

Hazel smiled broadly at Deric, excused herself, eased around him, and whispered, "Go get him, you silly cow! He might know who we're after!"

"But we don't know!" she said.

"No kidding. But he was one of them who was bashed, right? So maybe he does! So go get him and find out." She sneezed, fluffed her curls, adjusted her bosom. "This one is mine."

Confused, hurt that the redhead had immediately chosen Hazel over her, and distressed because she had the distinct feeling the world had jumped a peg and left her a hole behind, she shrugged into her coat, grabbed her purse, and finished her second drink in a gulp that had her eyes tearing, her throat burning, and her stomach feeling much better than it had in hours.

"And how badly did he hurt you, love?" Hazel cooed.

"Aw, not bad," Deric said.

"And did you see who did it?"

He nodded emphatically. "Damn right."

Janice hesitated.

Hazel cupped his cheek with one hand. "And what did this mean old basher look like, love?"

"Don't know."

Janice sucked in her lips to keep from smiling.

"You . . . don't know?"

"He was invisible, him."

"*Aha!*" shouted the blind man.

Hastily Janice lurched away on her heels. The redhead was obviously having Hazel on, and she wanted no part of it. Besides, if she didn't get a move on, she'd lose Kent Montana, which most probably wasn't his real name, him being a baron and all, but she had that instinctive policewoman's feeling that that's the way he wanted it. Which made him rather mysterious. And therefore somewhat attractive. And even if it was his real name, which it wasn't, he was still attractive and certainly the better of the bargain.

She stepped outside into the fog.

The muffled sounds of the traffic.

Do I really want to do this? she thought; couldn't I talk to him tomorrow? If he wants to make a complaint. Which I doubt, because he would have done so if he really wanted to. If he cared. Do I care? Is this what I signed up for, pretending to be a hooker and getting involved in pub fights?

The fog.

The flower girl singing sweetly in the dark.

She marched back inside, defiantly retook her place at the bar, and ordered a brandy. Hazel, ensconced on a bench with Deric, glared at her, but nothing more. And Janice figured that someone's quota would be met this night, unless the blonde slut turned out to be the jealous type.

"Hey, bitch!" Dora yelled as she returned from the Ladies.

Hazel moved.

Janice grinned.

If this was the worst the Festival could throw at her, she'd probably end up with Inspector Easewater's job.

"Eddie," Flora said to her barman, "do me a big favor, luv, and check to see if Mr. Smith's left his tray out yet. All this fuss made me forget. Go on now, there's a good boy."

Eddie Jones, having already lost the blonde hooker to the actor, and the brunette one to Deric, and the slut to the Ladies until she came back and nearly decapitated the brunette hooker, grumbled about slave labor in modern-day Britain and the perks of female companionship she was denying him, but nevertheless hurried out from behind the bar, through the side door to the stairwell, and up to the second landing, where, as usual, a battered wood tray with empty dishes sat. He picked it up after a spiteful but nonconnecting kick at the door, tried an unsuccessful peek through the dark keyhole, and dumped his burden into the sink downstairs.

"Beats me why you don't just toss him out," he complained.

"He pays his rent on time," Flora answered without missing a pump at the lager and beer handles.

"Bah! He makes more noise than this lot down here. No wonder you don't got more people up there."

"He likes his music."

"Like he likes his flippin' name," the barman muttered.

Flora jabbed his arm. "And what's that supposed to mean?"

Eddie looked the woman of his dreams full in the face, so closely that her heavenly eyes crossed until she leaned back. "You think he's really a Smith, Flora?" he said. "Come on, nobody's named Smith anymore." He lifted a soapy finger. "He's running from the coppers, that's what he's doin', hidin' up there, never showin' his bleedin' face. He's a killer or somethin', a spy or a Commie infiltrator.''

"Eddie, really!"

"Well, nothin' but trouble he's gonna be, you mark my words.''

She grinned and shook her head as she patted his cheek. "You're just too suspicious, Eddie, that's your problem.''

Right, he thought; but one of these days, he was going to get into that room and prove that the mysterious high-and-mighty Mr. Smith, what nobody ever saw except the first day he came in with all them crates and things, was up to no good. Then she'd believe him. She'd believe him then, when he was a proper hero and had captured the son of a bitch.

Then the hooker in the lamb's wool coat ordered a brandy, and he winked as he served her, wondering if she really believed no one knew she was a cop.

·3·

Merkleton was quiet.

The River George made its way darkly toward wherever it was going when it got there.

Traffic was smothered in billowing clouds of grey, all the neon smeared and hazed, all the pedestrians and partying Druids leaving the restaurants and cinema, the clubs and pubs, merely dark ghosts whose muffled footsteps were swallowed by the night.

It was wonderful.

He couldn't have asked for better protection.

He couldn't have asked for a better way to begin his Festival weekend.

It was as if he had been transported back in time, to that year when the Festival had given him his first taste of fame, to that magical night when that London agent had seen him, and heard him, and had whisked him away to riches and spangled coats.

Not even the fog had changed.

It was as if it had risen from the purifying waters of the River George just to be his silent accomplice, to wrap him in its arms and guide him through the medieval mazes of the streets, to blind others to him.

To lay them open to his desire.

To his will.

To his vengeance.

He hummed.

He laughed at the startled expression of a young waitress who had thought she was walking home alone.

He leaned against a brick wall and folded his arms across

his chest, in no hurry to choose his next victim.

The Festival had just begun.

He had all the time in the world.

All the time to spill all the blood he wanted.

He laughed aloud and listened to the echoes.

He sang a song he'd written just the night before and laughed again when an insomniac pigeon lost half its feathers.

Then he stepped away from the wall and spread his arms.

"Mine," he whispered into the fog, into the night. "Soon you will be all mine."

Red Moon Festival would never be the same.

He pictured a man. A very special man.

"Especially you," he vowed. "Especially you."

And then, from out of the depths of that foggy late September night, from what seemed to be all directions at once and no direction at all, in a voice coated with honey and hoarse with misused liquor, came the words of a waltz-time lament that, to all who heard it, reminded them of past loves and past lives and past mistakes and past triumphs; it also reminded them of a world-famous singer who, at the apex of his career, inexplicably vanished into the commercial void, leaving behind a fleeting legacy of false sightings, fifteen printings of his unauthorized biography, and not a single song to be recorded posthumously by American and Belgian country-and-western groups.

No one who heard it, and admittedly there weren't many, were unaffected:

> *I lost my heart to a chimney sweep,*
> *So I'm closin' the flue on you.*

One of those who did hear it took off his dark glasses, wiped his eyes, and proceeded to attempt to kick his effing accordion all the way to Trafalgar Square. He only got as far as the door to the King's Hump, however, before friendly hands took him by the shoulders and tossed him inside.

The pub closed shortly after that.

And Merkleton slept.

Slept, but not well.

~II~

The Festival

◆ 1 ◆

There were no gates at the entrance to Merkleton's park. One simply stepped from the bustle of the High Street onto a wide, peaceful blacktop path that led past ancient trees, well-tended grass, and blossoming rose gardens until the path split around a high and ornate Druidic fountain surrounded by low evergreen shrubs and a few stone benches for those too weary to move on. When the path rejoined itself, the land sloped gently downward, the trees eventually fell away, and the park transformed itself into Merkleton Green, an impressive expanse of lawn that overlooked the River George and the pleasure craft that plied it.

On the Green now, and flanking the path, dozens of local merchants and entrepreneurs hastily slapped the finishing touches on their bannered concession stands, shored up their peaked rainbow tents complete with wind-snapped pennants, and greased the gears on their tune-playing rides for the village children. In addition to all this joyful bustle, and as complement to it, there was an adequate white bandstand where a Salvation Army ensemble would soon fill the air with sprightly martial music, and down on the docks were boats of many sizes which would be launched for leisurely cruises up and down the waterway. Already, dozens of tourists and amazingly robed and hooded Druids were sampling wares, playing games, feeding the flotilla of ducks and geese, and resting on padded folding chairs to take in the sun that had driven the fog away.

It was Friday afternoon.

The Festival had begun.

And Claudius Cana chuckled as he stood midway up the

slope and looked down at the fools who were an unwitting part of his plan to conquer the world.

He was a portly man in a self-tailored black velvet tuxedo, sipping from a crystal champagne glass as he counted the crowd with eyes deeply set in a face more wrinkled than this morning's sheets. His thick, brushed-back hair was a distinguished shade of grey, his hands oddly slender for a man of his girth, and his voice, when raised, was hoarse enough to force his listeners to surreptitiously clear their throats.

A mink-trimmed vicuna topcoat was slung carelessly about his shoulders.

A fringed white scarf hung about his neck and lay flat across his chest.

In his right hand he gripped an ebony walking stick, its head made of silver and fashioned into the head of a howling wolf.

Beside him stood a woman, as slender as he was wide, as dark as he was light, white wine her drink of choice, her chic but unostentatious evening gown a sign that even the most expensive black cloth can look like cheap paint if it's tight enough, and the figure it hugs is round enough to incite a panic.

Her cigarette poked out of an engraved ivory holder, which she used now to point at two women impossibly dressed for the season strolling along the riverbank. It was the fifteenth time she had seen them. "I think they must like you, Claudius." Her black lipstick, when she smiled, made her teeth unnaturally white.

"Nonsense, Poetra," he said, though he swiveled his head around to watch them pass. In his voice, the faintest trace of an indefinable mid-European accent. "I have seen them before. I believe they are professionals."

Poetra Pioll held her breath, reached for her sequined purse. "Should we . . . ?"

He grinned at her. "Don't be silly. They are not of the police, you darling fool. I mean, they are . . . professionals."

"Oh," she said, hoisted her wineglass, and stared at the imported liquid within. "Oh."

He pointed at a short Druid in a purple robe, scurrying down the path toward the water. "Even fools like that have their needs, you know."

Languidly she blew smoke at the ceiling. "You fancy him too?"

He laughed, the sound like a hay-fever victim clearing his

sinuses. "You are precious, aren't you, my love?"

"It is my charm," she agreed.

The band cranked up.

A few people cheered.

A few Druids rolled a beer keg toward a rowboat.

Claudius beamed. For the eighth year in a row he had been elected Festival chairman, and for the eighth year in a row it was evident that Merkleton would prosper and be well under his expert direction.

But what Merkleton didn't know was that this was Cana's last year at his post. If all went well, by Sunday afternoon he would be in possession of such treasure that the Queen Herself would whimper in envy and he could close down his tailor shop forever. And once that treasure was his, only Death would have the power to prevent him from conquering the known civilized world.

A strolling constable passed them and saluted them with his nightstick.

Claudius nodded back and checked his watch. "We will give her another ten minutes, I think. Longer than that, and I fear that we have lost what we have so recently found."

Poetra paled, a feat of conjuration that terrified a nearby vicar into believing he'd seen a ghost. "You can't mean that," she said huskily. "We cannot lose her now! Not after all this time!"

The large man patted her trembling hand. "Not to worry, my love. I meant only temporarily. We can always find her again. She is not all that clever, not nearly as clever as I."

"But how?" she demanded. "It took us this long to track her here. If we—"

He hushed her with a look that brought his white eyebrows together over the broad bridge of his flush-tipped nose. "You are working yourself into a state," he cautioned sternly. "This cannot be. You must control yourself, Poetra, or all is lost."

She nodded, and closed her eyes.

A young black-haired woman in a skimpy white sacrificial robe ran between the tents, shrieking with laughter as tourists and Druids pelted after her; two constables chatted with a burly man distinguished by the monocle he couldn't manage to keep in his right eye; ducks rose in a flutter from the river, calling, wheeling, and settling again.

The scent of food, beer, wine, sweat, sex, grass, trees, a few loose dogs, the mud flats, perfume.

Barbaric, he thought disdainfully. But then, this whole country was barbaric, still struggling to climb from the depths of its barbaric beginnings and failing utterly, miserably, and thus rendering itself perfect for the hunters and snipers of the real world.

A world which he, the master of all he surveyed and a bit that he hadn't seen yet, would soon tuck into his voluminous hip pocket and sit on if he wanted to because none would dare oppose him, and even if they did, they wouldn't be able to because they wouldn't know who they were opposing.

It was perfect.

It was the culmination of a dream he'd had since a year ago last summer, when he'd taken his holiday in Y——, heard curious stories about a mysterious man holed up in a deserted farmhouse, discovered who that man was, and, most importantly, discovered what that man had.

He checked his watch again.

Soon.

Very soon.

And if not very soon, pretty soon.

Poetra completed her calming exercise and shook her head gently. "I am better," she announced. She tapped him with her holder, then leaned over and brushed the ashes from his sleeve. "A penny for your thoughts."

He blinked once, very slowly, and said, "It is funny, my sweet lover, but the moment you asked me that question, the name of an old friend—and I use the word so loosely, it immediately takes on its opposite meaning—popped into my mind."

"Oh? And who might that be?"

He smiled. "You wouldn't know him."

"I know everyone," she boasted.

"Do you know a man named Kent Montana?"

Poetra gasped, unconsciously made the sign of the cross, and gasped again when she realized what she had done and didn't know how to counteract it, so she drank her wine instead and sneered at the tourists. "Good heavens, what made you think of . . . him?"

"I don't know," he answered truthfully.

"Then please, don't do it again."

"Very well."

"Thank you."

The band finished its first selection to much applause and throwing of money.

The two professionals sat on the riverbank and pulled off their shoes.

A little girl threw up on the purple Druid.

Claudius looked at his watch and sighed. She wasn't coming. His man had assured him she would probably be here, but clearly he was wrong. Claudius decided to have the man killed as soon as he took over the world.

Yet he worried not, nor did he fret.

He knew she was in town. Somewhere. And Merkleton wasn't so large that he wouldn't be able to find her.

He hummed to himself, took Poetra's arm, and formed his own little procession down into the masses, into the adulation that washed over him, as was his due.

"The hell with it," he whispered to her as he nodded to the vicar. "When we find that damned bitch, you can tear off her head."

"Oh god," Poetra gasped. "Oh god, Claudius . . . thank you!"

Milo Yonker threw himself into the river.

It had been bad enough that the only robe he'd been able to get hold of was a garish sort of purple, even if it did have the tasteful gold trim glittering around hood and hem; now he had to deal with the disgusting aftermath of a little girl's obsession with Dutch chocolate and ice-cold milk. It didn't bear thinking about what would happen if his costume didn't come clean. At the very least, Gretchen and Kirkie would throw him over for a couple of wealthy tourists with automatic cameras. And what they would do then absolutely didn't bear thinking about at all.

He sputtered, he stroked, he reached the far bank and swam back, the current not powerful enough to give him any problems, the boats sweeping up and down giving him wide berth because he looked like nothing more than a drenched weasel in purple trying to catch a tasty goose. When he reached the shore, he fell onto the grass, rolled onto his back, and stared at the sky.

The breeze chilled him.

So did his thoughts.

The Festival was not turning out the way he had hoped, the way he had planned for so many months.

In the first place, Gretchen was having altogether too much fun in her skimpy white sacrificial costume, not even bothering to pretend to be the terrified virgin slated for heart-cutting on Saturday night; in the second place, Kirkie couldn't keep her hands off him, which at other times wouldn't have been a problem, except that a purple Druid was supposed to be one of great rank, and therefore above public displays of licentiousness; he had hoped for a plain brown wrapper to give him anonymity, but they'd all been taken.

And in the third place, he had spotted Kent Montana the night before, staggering through the fog back to the Hotel Bowlingham, and if Milo wanted his scheme to work, the one thing he didn't need was a snoopy old baron screwing up his life.

That didn't bear thinking about.

He sighed.

He cupped his hands behind his head.

He watched a duck dive-bomb a fellow Druid.

It all depended on the most precise timing. If that failed, he would fail; if he failed, the scheme would fail; if the scheme failed, he would be back behind the counter of his fish 'n' chips shop quicker than you can say Willie Nelson's a fag. And smelling all that fish, all that batter, all that soggy newsprint one more day was something that, God love him, didn't bear thinking about.

He had to succeed.

Merkleton was not, could not, be the end of his world.

"Resting, O Mighty One?"

He turned his head. Kirkie Algood, wearing a billowing green robe with white trim about the hood and hem, sat cross-legged beside him. She winked. Her freckles were appealingly dark, her nose appealingly blunt, her startling green eyes narrowed in a way that made Milo sit up and cross his legs in a hurry.

"I'm thinking."

"You're wet."

"I fell in the river."

Her nose wrinkled.

Gretchen sprinted by, pursued by a pair of Germans.

"Slut," Kirkie sneered, her left hand fluttering until it came to rest on his thigh.

"That as may be," he said, "but we still need her."

She snorted; her hand jerked.

Unfortunately it was true. Aside from being the sacrifice, it was Gretchen Wain, who, whilst on a brisk walking tour through Y——a year ago last summer, had spotted Milo's singing idol, even though the rest of the country believed him long dead. She had also spotted what the man had given to a frumpy-looking woman working in the local library.

She was the only one who could identify that woman.

Without her, Milo was lost.

Unless the man he had hired could locate the woman, in which case Gretchen was superfluous. Except as the sacrifice. And without the sacrifice, there would be no Festival grand finale. And if there was no Festival grand finale—well, hell, that didn't bear thinking about.

Kirkie's hand inserted itself in a fold and tried to straighten it out.

He plucked the hand away and placed it primly in her lap. "Darling, you're not paying attention."

She shrugged. "Seems to me, love, that you're the one who keeps going off into thoughtful reveries. Besides, I'm bored. This Festival is boring. This whole weekend is a flop!"

He smiled knowingly. "Not if we're successful."

Her glum expression brightened. "Oh! Yeah!"

"And if we are . . . ?"

She clapped her hands.

Gretchen ran back the other way, the Germans replaced by a trio of Italians.

"If we are, we're rich." She leaned forward. "Very rich." She kissed his cheek. "Disgustingly rich." She caressed the side of his neck. "Obscenely rich."

He pulled away before she unearthed another adjective, and another fold. When she pouted annoyance, he rose with as much dignity as his sodden robe could provide and assisted her to her feet. Then he adjusted his sodden hood so that no one could see his face. "Listen," he said, guiding her along the path toward the oak grove at the Green's far end, "the only problem is—"

"Problem? What problem? Damnit, Milo, you swore to me

there wouldn't be any problems." She stopped. "Oh my god, you haven't got the stuff yet, have you?"

"No," he admitted. "But I haven't seen my man yet either."

"Have you looked for him?"

"I've been in the river."

"All day?"

"And drying out. Don't forget the drying out."

She rolled her eyes, stamped her foot. "Damnit, Milo, if you don't have that stuff by tonight, I'll . . . I'll . . . I'll—"

"Don't say it," he said.

"—leave you."

He sighed and walked on, passing two hookers and marveling at how tight a tartan miniskirt could get.

Kirkie snarled.

He hurried on, past tents filled with long tables and hungry customers, an open shed with a lopsided roulette wheel, and a small corral where small animals were petted and tortured by small children. Once beyond that, the crowd thinned, and he climbed the slope a few yards before turning around to face the river, paying no attention to the water dripping from his hem to the grass.

Kirkie remained on the path.

He beckoned.

Gretchen barreled past, the trio of Italians replaced by a quartet of leather-jacketed teenage boys.

Kirkie tripped her.

The boys caught her.

Milo sighed and hoped the swim in the river hadn't ruined his voice the way it had his robe. If it had, they were all ruined; if it hadn't, it might be ruined anyway, by the way Gretchen was shrieking and those cops over there were looking her way.

Lord, that didn't bear thinking about, not in the least.

He sighed again and blessed a company of old French women who mistook him for a friar.

But enough of this *angst*, he ordered; get it together, Milo old son, and think of the future.

What was important now, aside from getting the hell out of his dripping robe, was to make sure he received the goods before tomorrow night. He needed time to practice. He needed time to tune up.

He needed to contact his man right away, before Kirkie learned what he really intended to do.

If she found out prematurely, it won't be no virgin what's chopped up tomorrow.

A rowboat drifted at anchor on the river.

It bobbed in the wakes of passing craft, swung about its chain when the breeze gusted, settled on the dark surface, waiting to begin its dance once again.

A duck landed on the stern and began preening itself.

A sudden humming.

The duck fled.

A low and hearty laugh that soon turned to a cackling.

"I've had it, Janice. I'm tired, I'm hungry, I'm footsore, I'm—"

"Discouraged."

"All this money, all these tourists, and all they can think about is chasing Druids, for god's sake."

"Maybe," Janice said, her shoes in one hand, "Druids didn't have hookers."

Hazel only shrugged. Then she gestured with her own shoes up the path toward the trees. "I think we'll go back to the Hump tonight."

"Who? Deric?"

Hazel stared. "What?"

Janice blushed.

"Jesus, woman, jump in the river, will you? I'm talking about returning to the scene of the crime." She lowered her voice and winked at the vicar. "Listen, don't you think it's rather odd that no one made a report of that attack? I checked. It's like it never happened, like."

"Why is that odd? No one was seriously hurt, nothing was broken but a stupid fruit machine, and if we show up again, they'll really think we're hookers."

"We are."

"Well, yes, but no, if you know what I mean."

"God help me," Hazel said, "but I do. I really do."

"So are we going?"

"You want to spend the night alone? In your flat? Soaking your feet while crime strikes again?"

"Crime?"

"Another attack, Janice. Suppose there's another attack and we're not there?"

"My feet are fine."

The vicar passed them again and held up a Bible.

Hazel grabbed her arm. "Let's go find the inspector and tell him we're working a double shift. There's something about that place I don't like, love. There's just something about it."

"What attack?"

Kent stood at the tree line and leaned against a venerable drooping oak, watching the festivities with a sad smile twitching his lips. It would be dark soon; he could tell that by the way the sun had begun to work itself below the horizon upriver. And then the lights would come on, the pubs and clubs would fill, and he would be no nearer employment than he had been that morning.

Most of the day, when he should have been enjoying himself with the other townspeople, eating and drinking and making a royal fool of himself, had been spent in his empty room on the balky telephone, trying to get in touch with his equally balky agent while nursing a hangover that made the Salvation Army brass seem like harps. To no avail, on both counts. The rest of the day had then been spent in his empty room dismantling a letter bomb his mother had sent him in the afternoon post. He knew it was a bomb because of the ticking—she always used the same damn clock, having bought them by the lot; he knew it was from his mother because the letter was ostensibly a birthday card, the object of which wasn't due for another seven months.

Beside, she used her own return address.

The woman had no shame.

Once it was defused and disposed of, and glad he was that he had had a great deal of practice and his mother was no more imaginative than she ever was, he had eaten in the Bowlingham restaurant, napped in his empty room, and had finally dressed in tweed jacket, sweater, jeans, and running shoes, and had walked down to the park, just as the day's events were drawing to a close.

The story, he thought mournfully, of his baronial life.

His right hand gingerly touched the swelling at the base of his skull.

That too.

He watched with some amusement Claudius Cana and that zombie girlfriend of his parading around the Green as if he

were the Lord Mayor; he watched with shoulders shaking with
silent laughter as Gretchen Wain, looking damn stupid in a
skimpy white sacrificial costume, allowed herself to be chased
by every man with two working legs, and one determined
pensioner with a retractable cane; he shook his head in amazement at the two hookers he'd seen the night before, now trudg-
ing barefoot along the riverbank and clearly not having any
luck at all.

And, as he listened to the children squealing their delight
on the rides and in the petting zoo, he began to wonder, as the
shadows grew long and a light mist hovered above the river's
surface, if perhaps he had been wrong.

Perhaps he ought not to try to find a new part at all.

Perhaps he ought to settle down.

Here.

In Merkleton.

Open a nostalgia shop or something and bilk the tourists,
just like everyone else. Spend his evenings at the King's Hump,
flirting with Flora, sparring with Eddie, and figuring out ways
to stop Zero from getting a new accordion without hurting his
feelings.

There were worse ways to spend one's life.

Worse ways indeed.

He pushed away from the tree and headed back toward the
High Street.

A nanny nearly ran him down with her pram and the four
toothsome toddlers racing behind her.

A constable eyed him warily.

Gretchen flew past, screaming at a pursuing American that
she was saving herself for the virgin sacrifice.

His head throbbed for a moment.

And as he touched the swelling again, he decided not to be
hasty. After all, he had been assaulted. And he still wasn't
convinced—call it a gut feeling, instinct, preservation reaction,
distrust of easy answers, the steel pipe still in his coat, which
hung in the wardrobe of his empty hotel room—that the attack
had been a random one.

And until he proved or disproved that gut feeling, that instinct, that preservation reaction, he would not be able to rest
easy. He certainly wouldn't be able to open a nostalgia shop.

No.

He would wait before he made his final decision.

Especially when something made him shiver without warning—instinct, gut feeling, whatever the hell—and he looked
over his shoulder.

There, following him up the path, was a thick cloud of fog.

Night had come again.

To Merkleton.

England.

And Kent Montana knew his life would never be the same.

✦ 2 ✦

Shortly after sunset, deep in the alley, huddled against the damp, the little flower girl of Rains Lane decided that she no longer wanted to sell her wares that night.

Instead, she wanted to go home.

The place . . . her place . . . was haunted.

Songs were sung with no one to sing them; footsteps followed her with no one to make them; the rasp of harsh breathing that echoed off the buildings.

Haunted.

The Lane was haunted.

Ordinarily she prided herself on being a fairly level-handed lass, not easily given to seeing shadows where there was no light, or seduced by ghosts and monsters born of the mark of her imagination.

But this wasn't her imagination.

This was definitely no place to be tonight. Perhaps tomorrow, when the Festival reached its climax and the village streets were packed with revelers and police.

But not tonight.

Tonight the Lane was haunted.

Quickly she snuggled her shawl more closely about her neck, tucked her basket under her arm, and fled as best she could through the fog.

Something touched her cheek.

She whimpered, spun, saw nothing.

Something touched her again.

"Who . . . who's there?" she called timidly.

A husky laugh in her right ear.

"Who . . . ?"

Something gently tweaked her shoulder.

With eyes nearly closed in terror, she bit down on her lip and tried to run again, feeling the fog-weighted shawl slap against her back, hearing her worn pumps slip and slap against the cobbles.

A cackling laugh in her left ear.

She ran harder, not caring if her flowers spilled from the basket into the puddles and alley glop, not caring if someone saw her fleeing and laughed.

Oh God, she prayed; oh God, please don't let me die.

She tripped and almost fell, cried out softly until she regained her balance. The basket dropped from her grasp, and she reached for it instinctively, clasped it to her bosom, and with a wild look behind her, ran on.

Soon enough she was on the High Street, surrounded by light however hazy and distant, in the midst of pedestrians hurrying toward the warmth of their homes and their loved ones, or the parties that by their nature excluded the likes of her. She paused to take a breath, then ran on.

Behind her, in the dark, in the fog, someone laughed.

· 3 ·

Fearfully, trepidatiously, Lizzy Howgath took what she had come to consider was her customary table at the King's Hump, fully aware that people would talk, and not caring. For tonight had to be the night. Time was running out, and Merkleton, not to mention the rest of England, was fast approaching the end of its rope, the end of the line, the last call, the last trump, the last ding of the dinner bell.

She must succeed now; or else.

But, as she set her heavy shopping bag between her feet for safekeeping, she saw no one among tonight's patrons who answered the description of the man for whom she had been searching all these weeks.

Of course, the object of her search could well have been the aristocratic gentleman she had seen the previous evening, the one with the awful hat. But the chances of him walking in again, after being so viciously attacked, were virtually nil, and she dared not believe in miracles. After all, she wasn't stupid. She worked in a library. She read books. She knew full well that a victim seldom returned to the scene of his severe beating, at least not within twenty-four hours of same. It just wasn't done.

Nudging the bag with her knees, feeling the weight of her burden press against her flesh, she made sure that slimy little bald man wasn't hanging around, and stared at the pint of lager she cupped between her hands.

Time.

So little time.

Dear Lord, she prayed, let this be the night.

"Excuse me," a young man interrupted, standing over her

table with a mug in one hand and a chair in the other. "Is this seat taken?"

She crossed her eyes.

He staggered away.

She took a long sip and wondered if she had done the right thing, scaring him off like that. If the man she sought didn't show this night, she would have to stop being so choosy and pick the first one she believed might have a prayer against the horror that as yet had not been revealed to the world. She knew she would be sending him to certain doom, so potent was the information she carried, but there was no other way.

She could do nothing on her own.

A tear stung her eye.

The young man with the chair returned. "Pardon me, miss, but I couldn't help noticing that you seem distressed."

"Oh, I am," she said apologetically.

"Mayhaps I may be of some small assistance." His smile was kind; his face almost painfully handsome; his outfit several complementary shades of pleasant forest green, though it did not disguise the fact that he was extraordinarily well muscled for a blond man in a pub. "It may sound silly, it certainly has to some others, but I am what you call a hero by trade. Nobody believes it, of course. Not even my old horse, Bill, who might look like a white elephant to the untrained eye, but he's actually quite the equine when he puts his mind to it."

She glanced around.

There was no elephant in the pub.

And the man had a distinct American accent.

"At any rate," he continued in the most engaging manner, "I'm not averse to rescuing beautiful women in red coats from dangerous situations. As long as there is a dangerous situation. I'm not much good at the other stuff. Quite frankly it's a pain in the ass, being a hero. But that's what I do, and that's what I am, so if I can help . . . ?"

Suddenly Lizzy brightened. The man was quite obviously out of his mind, maybe even severely jet-lagged, but to give him his due, perhaps she did need some American brashness about now, American know-all, American courage, American soul. If her chosen one didn't show up, yes, this could be the one.

Naturally he wouldn't survive; but death comes to us all,

doesn't it, so why worry about it, why concern ourselves with
all the blood and the shattered bones and—

Lizzy! she thought, you're doing it again.

"Please," she offered with a magnanimous gesture, "I don't
mean to be rude. Do have a seat."

He held up the chair. He put it down. He sat. He flexed. He
called out to the blind man whistling "Dixie" at the door to
make sure his elephant didn't wander off in the fog. Then he
held out his hand. "Dove," he said gently.

"Oh my," she replied, feeling a blush work its way to her
warm cheeks.

He seemed puzzled. Then he smiled in quaint embarrass-
ment. "Oh. No. No, I didn't mean that you were a dove, miss.
Not that you aren't, of course. And a beautiful one, at that,
although I've never seen a red one. But that's my name. Dove.
Me and my faithful horse, Bill, at your service."

Blushing more furiously now at the *faux pas* she had made,
she covered her social ineptitude by emptying her glass and
waving it around until the harried barman saw her and brought
another to the table.

Dove watched her carefully.

She sipped.

She wiped her lips.

She nodded that she was ready.

"Okay," he said, smiling. "So tell me, miss, what's the
story so far?"

Lizzy held her breath.

"Well," she began at last, when the American appeared to
be getting nervous, "you're not going to believe this."

Kent ate.

Temporarily setting aside his plans to settle down, he called
his agent at home and was told by the man's mistress that the
sonofabitch was having dinner with his wife.

He paced his room until he started colliding with the walls;
he watched two hours of a snooker tournament on the television
attached to the wardrobe, then decided, when he found himself
fascinated by the hushed commentary, that he might as well
go crazy at the pub; at least there he'd have company. So
thinking, he changed his sweater, changed his jeans, polished
his boots, and rode down in the impossibly small elevator to
the lobby. The residents' bar was jammed again, Druids and

the town council throwing sacrificial darts at enlarged photographs of Stonehenge. He shook his head and stepped outside, hesitating under the hotel's square marquee while he examined the fog.

It was thicker tonight, more chilled, and had turned the world black and white, turned the traffic to ghosts, and the pedestrians to spirits who were having a grand time despite the disheartening weather.

With a sigh better suited to the suitor of a lost love, he headed for Rains Lane, surprising himself by hoping that the blonde hooker might be there. A snort. He should be ashamed of himself. But failing that, there was always Dora Feathers, who knew more about royalty than her Deric ever suspected.

"Evening, m'lord," Zero Zuller greeted when he reached the entrance. "Been thinking about my new accordion?"

Kent tapped his shoulder. "Keep those lips pursed, lad. Makes you a better kisser."

Zero's laugh was sarcastic, and he waved Kent inside.

This time he was no stranger—there were loud hellos and doffed caps as he made his way to the far end of the bar. Flora, he noted, had already replaced the fruit machine; Deric was in a dark corner, alone, glaring at nothing with the eyes of a man too drunk to realize that his pants were falling down; Eddie seemed in a particularly foul mood, grabbing up coins like he was trying to pull out someone's hair; and by george and stone the crows, over there against the wall were the two hookers, blonde and brunette.

He pretended not to notice.

"So look, but don't touch," Flora warned.

"Wouldn't think of it."

"Of course not, m'lord." And she giggled as she poured him a generous portion of Glenbannock.

He stared at the glass. "What's this?"

"Your expression, m'lord. You look like hell. If I get you drunk enough, you won't need to bother about the likes of them over there."

Kent toasted her with a mock leer.

She slapped him lightly with a towel.

He settled against the wall and unobtrusively watched the lamb's wool blonde as she tried not to watch him. He scolded himself for thinking what he was thinking, emptied his glass, and poured another from the fresh bottle. When he looked up, she was pointedly not looking back, and he almost laughed aloud.

My lord, he thought, this could be interesting.

Eddie the barman yelled at someone for spilling lager on the floor, and Flora told him to cork it, bottle it, and stow it on the shelf. He snarled. She pinched his thigh so hard his face went red, then white.

Trouble in paradise, Kent thought, wondering what had come between them. Eddie clearly had the wind up about something, and Flora was just as clearly on the defensive.

The blonde was still not watching him.

A Druid came in, asking for sacrificial volunteers, and was hooted back into the fog, where he cursed the building, the patrons, and all the liquor therein.

A few of the regulars noted that the time now was just about the time when Kent was bashed last night.

He took another drink.

The blonde didn't watch him.

This, he told himself, is ridiculous. You're a grown man, laddie. You don't need Dutch courage to talk to a woman, even one in her position, sitting against the wall.

Half an hour later, he had just found the nerve to convince himself that holding an innocent conversation with a woman wasn't the same as doing anything wrong in his empty hotel room, when a gang of party-hoppers poured in from the Lane, calling for drinks all around, crowding the locals away from the bar, and dumping so much money and traveler's checks into Eddie's hands that he stopped bothering to count it and simply dumped it into the till.

Swell, he thought; with all that money floating around so freely, what chance did he, a baron without a part, have?

Of course, he could always hope to be attacked again. Then she would come to his aid, bathe his face, tend his bruises, cover him with kindness of a sort he hadn't experienced since the time he'd learned a few tricks from the cook at the island orphanage, who knew things about ladles his mother never suspected.

Ha.

Fat chance.

"Sir?"

He blinked.

He started.

He snapped his head back and slammed it against the wall.

"Oh dear," the blonde said, slipping her warm hand compassionately behind his head. "I didn't mean to startle you."

"Not at all," he answered graciously. "I was just startled, that's all."

"Oh good."

He smiled.

She smiled.

He wiped a hand across his face to realign his vision and glanced over her shoulder, where her partner had engaged Deric in some serious conversation. "Nice evening."

"My feet hurt."

"I beg your pardon?"

The woman held up the red pumps she carried in her right hand. "My feet hurt. I've been walking all day."

I'll bet, he thought, without a trace of rancor.

"You know," she said, "I didn't think you'd be here. I mean, I was kind of hoping you would—"

"You were?"

"—but seeing as how you were so brutally assaulted on this very spot, and seeing as how the perpetrator escaped without notice except for the blind man who claimed he was invisible— the perpetrator, not the blind man—I must admire your courage for returning to the scene of the crime."

"You're drunk," he said mildly.

"Did you understand me?"

He nodded.

"Then we're even, aren't we?"

Dear lord, he thought; dear lord.

Then the lights went out.

And somebody screamed.

"Oh no, you don't!" Flora shouted, and the pub was flooded with light again, blinding white streams of it from lanterns she and Eddie had attached that morning to the rim of the glass racks along the length of the bar.

But it was too late.

During the brief dark interlude, something hard had slammed against the back of Kent's head.

His lights went out again.

Zero bellowed for the army, Hazel bellowed for the police, Dora bellowed for vengeance, and Kent sat on the floor, waiting for the pain and the noise and the gorgeous legs at eye level to come back into focus. When they did, he allowed himself to be assisted to his feet, allowed Flora to pour him another glass of Glenbannock, and allowed as how his suspicions appeared to be correct.

"What suspicions?" the blonde asked quickly.

"It would appear, my dear, that I am no random target."

"That's because you were holding still."

The party folk cleared out.

Deric slumped over his table while Dora massaged his neck.

The woman in red sprinted out the exit, leaving behind a rather bewildered young man in green who kept grabbing for people and demanding they be quiet so his elephant wouldn't bolt and leave him in this place, wherever the hell it was.

Kent knew the feeling; he was a bit lost himself.

Then Zero ran up and said, "Now, this time, m'lord, you have to believe me."

"Invisible," he said flatly.

The blind man nodded, looked to the hooker, and nodded again. "Clear as the nose on your face."

"And he's gone again."

"Absolutely."

Kent fumbled in his pockets until he found a ten-pound note. He slapped it into Zero's hand, slipped his arm around the blonde, and said, "Keep this up, mate, you'll be able to buy your own accordion. Assuming my head doesn't fall off."

Zero grabbed him as he tried to leave. "But m'lord—"

Kent pulled away his arm, with a look that quieted the entire room and half the block. They knew that expression, the set of his shoulders, the lift of his granite chin; they knew it all too well, and no one denied him when he walked into the fog, the woman at his side.

No one said a word.

Kent Montana was angry.

◆ 4 ◆

Etta Numm, stalwart and solid coproprietor of Ringstone Foods and Take-away Sandwiches, stood on the sidewalk and counted the oranges left in their canted display crates. When she finished, she counted the cabbages, the heads of lettuce, the bunches of bananas, and the grapes. Then she rolled up her sleeves and began stacking the crates one atop the other, to carry into the grocery so she and her partner could close up for the night.

No sense in staying open. All this damn fog, people screaming and running about, it fair put all their customers off their feed. Not to mention his lordship and that harlot, right out there in the middle of the street, walking along sweet as you please, just like they belonged to polite society. She'd never thought it of him, not a man of his breeding and being a star in America and all. Their passing had fair knocked her off her bunion-plagued feet. No; no sense in it tonight. Might as well pack it in and go home where it was warm.

"Etta!" Ethel Queen called from behind the register cleverly placed by the door to discourage shoplifters.

"What!"

"How much is the spinach?"

Etta sighed and poked her head inside. "We ain't got spinach, Ethel dear." She smiled massively at the customer, an elderly gentleman who tipped his hat to her.

"What's this, then?" Ethel asked.

She squinted. "Looks like spinach."

"Then how much is it?"

"Don't know. We don't carry spinach. Never have, never will. You get iron," she explained to the gentleman, "but you

57

get gas as well. Got to boil the brains out of it first.''

"Etta, for heaven's sake.''

Etta shrugged and returned outside, tugging her ancient cardigan around rugby-trained shoulders, stamping her booted feet to kick-start her circulation, and thumbing from her mottled brow several damp strands of hair that had escaped the netting. Then she slapped her hands on her hips and glared at the fruit and veggies, daring them to roll from their canted perches. They did that sometimes, she knew; a heavy lorry, a row of cabs, and the next thing was a hail of free food spilling into the gutter.

They didn't move.

She snorted, readjusted her sweater, and began stacking.

"Etta!''

"What!''

"You left the radio on in back!''

"Didn't have it on!''

"Well, it's on now!''

Etta jabbed a finger at her work, pinning it in place, and stalked inside.

The shop was small, split in half at the front by a long shelf divider that held the biscuits, the candy, fourteen varieties of crisps, and eight different sizes of battery. The lefthand wall held the magazines, all the dirty ones on top so only the tallest or most determined filthy-minded men could reach them. That was her idea; Ethel had wanted them near the register so she could keep up with British morals.

"I don't hear nothing," she said.

"Well, I did."

Sighing to prove she was only doing this out of practiced martyrdom, she trundled down the left aisle to the workroom that passed as their office, and looked at the radio sitting on the school desk Ethel had pinched from her nephew.

The radio was off.

"It's off!'' she bellowed as she returned to the front.

Ethel, who spent most of her waking hours denying that she looked like her pet bulldog, Archie—without any success to anyone who had seen the bulldog slobbering and snoring behind the counter—shook her head in doubt. "I heard it. Clear as you, I heard it.''

"Well, it ain't on.''

"Playing one of them tunes you like.''

Etta scowled. She had told the silly cow a hundred times she didn't like *tunes*; she liked life-mirroring *ballads*, sad ones about railroad men losing their women to sweet-tongued Irish salesmen, and women losing their men to fire-haired beauties from the wild mountains above Loch Ness. True they were; life as it was lived, not as the faggot rockers would have it. Many a tear had fallen in her room late at night as she knitted a new sweater for her budgie and listened to real singers like that Welsh old-timer Racig Dargren pump the hell out of a heartbreak. Ethel, on the other hand, curled up in her room with that smelly bulldog and Radio Free Europe.

A wonder, she thought, they'd stayed together all these years, two widows whose husbands had died in the cheese riots of 1956. At least that's what the police had told them. All very hush-hush. Heroes they were. And that too prompted a tear or three on occasion.

"Well," she said, huffing back to the door, "it's off, and that's that."

Ethel shrugged, snuffled, bit off the end of a panatela, and lit it. "Must've been my imagination."

Etta's reply would have been cutting and suitably disdainful, as close to mocking as she could get without pissing off the bulldog, had it not been preempted by a shattering crash in back, by the frozen food and Swiss cheese. Immediately, she ducked around the center display, arms wide to catch the culprit.

Then she remembered that no one had been there when she'd gone to the office.

Yet there on the floor were soda cans rolling slowly around, a split carton of orange juice, busted boxes of cake mix, and what looked like . . . no, it couldn't be . . . what looked like . . .

Etta fainted.

Ethel screamed.

And a hooker leapt through the doorway and shouted, "All right, all right, what's all the fuss?"

Angus Dean prided himself on his stealth, even if he didn't lurk all that well. But the skirt in the abominable red coat wasn't doing him any favors. As soon as she had bolted from the pub, she'd clattered off down the Lane, heading away from the main street as if every demon in denim was at her heels; and though he was more than able to keep her in sight because

of the brilliance of her garment, it didn't require a hell of a lot
of stealth.

She made too much noise, for one thing. He could be wearing
hobnails and full armor, and she wouldn't have heard him
sitting on her bloody shoulder.

For another, she kept falling down.

Now, granted, the worn cobbles and loose paving stones
were slick and slippery from all the fog; and granted, the drinks
she had had with that Robin Hood bloke, not to mention those
she had had before, probably made navigation difficult; but
this bordered on the ridiculous.

Every ten steps without fail she dropped onto her rump.

And every ten steps behind her, just out of sight in the fog,
he had to stop and hold his breath while she scrambled to her
feet, picked up that shopping bag, and started off again, the
bag clutched to her chest while her free hand brushed off the
back of her coat.

Ten steps.

Thump.

Ten steps.

Thump.

He had to give it to her, though. Nary a word or a whimper
did she utter. Down, up, and onward without so much as a
squeal. A spunky lass, that one; a credit to her not inconsiderable sex. Yet, by the time they reached the Lane's end,
it was all he could do to keep from flinging himself at her,
picking her up, and carrying her to wherever she was heading
in such a god-awful hurry except for all the falling down.

It was a shame he hadn't had troopers like her when he was
serving. A damned shame.

A few moments later she paused without warning. A birdlike
glance left and right, a terrified check over her shoulder, and
she was off. Hastening across a postage-stamp park which,
thanks to the combined wisdom of nature activists and the
government, had been covered with concrete save for tiny ovals
of earth out of which grew trees despairing of ever seeing a
full day's sun.

The fog thickened slightly.

Angus tripped over a bench, a trash bin, a sleeping wino,
and a naked pigeon.

Still the woman hove on.

Ten steps; thump.

The concrete was slippery too.

At the far end she fell off the curb, and he could stand it no longer. The woman would be the death of him before midnight. As she punched the curbing in silent frustration, he stepped out of the fog, grabbed her arm, and hauled her to her feet.

"Miss," he said before she could scream, "you're going to kill yourself before you reach the end of the block."

"Oh Lord," she gasped, and hugged the bag to her breast. "Are you going to rape me?"

He laughed. "No, miss, not me. I'm just a poor sailor wandering about this miserable town." A wave of his hand. "The fog turned me around some."

Her smile made his back straighten, his heart pitter, and his blood pat.

"It's these silly shoes," she said. "I just can't seem to get the hang of them. I've been shopping, you know. You can tell by this bag, I guess. That makes it pretty clear, wouldn't you say if you didn't know me? That I've been shopping, that is. Not for the shoes, though. They're the only ones I could—oh dear, am I talking too much?"

Like robins in spring, larks in summer, nightingales in Berkeley Square, he thought in a rush of rusty poetry that made his chin tremble.

"Sergeant Major Angus Dean, retired, at your service," he blurted at the incredible but true twinkle in her eye.

"Lizzy Howgath," she said shyly. "I thought you were a sailor."

"The fog," he answered quickly, "is very confusing."

"Indeed."

Before he knew it, then, her hand took his arm in a dizzyingly proprietary fashion, and they started across a narrow empty street. No lights in any of the apartment-block windows. Only the occasional fuzz of a streetlamp along the way to the next corner. She slipped ten steps later. He caught her. She apologized for her clumsiness.

"Allow me," he said, reached down, snatched off her shoes, broke off the heels cleanly, and slipped the shoes back on whilst still on his soggy knees. "A trick I learned in the Sudan," he explained.

She giggled. "Sergeant Major, unless you intend to propose, I think you'd better get up."

"Marry me," he replied instantly.

She giggled again. "But I hardly know you, Angus."

He stood and put her hand on his arm once more, looked down as they made it safely to the next sidewalk, and said, "We've our whole lives to get to know each other, Lizzy."

When she blushed, he nearly shouted with joy; when she hugged his hand to her side and he felt the flesh beneath the red coat, he broke out in a gallant sweat; when she allowed as how she was rather a klutz when it came to taking care of herself even if she was a terribly efficient and highly rated librarian, he was ready to tell his bosses to take a flying leap off the nearest bridge.

This was no woman to be following on a dark and foggy night.

This was no woman to be entangled in a web of intrigue and possible murder.

No; this was *his* woman now; and make no mistake about it, she had the full force of Angus Dean forever on her side.

"So," he said with gentle gruffness, "what were you doing in that terrible place back there?"

She averted her face. "You . . . saw?"

"I couldn't help myself."

"I was . . . hiding."

Damn, he thought; jealous husband or angry boyfriend. I knew it was too good to last. The story of my misbegotten life.

Suddenly, under the soft waterfall of light from an ornate streetlamp, she stopped and turned to face him. "Angus, can I trust you?"

"With your life," he vowed.

"Oh dear."

"But it won't come to that," he told her tenderly.

"Don't be too sure," she answered with a quick look in the direction they had just traveled.

"What? A woman such as yourself in peril of her life?" He laughed heartily, but softly. "Lizzy, that can't be true."

Her eyes downcast, her chin quivering, she nodded. "It is, Angus. I have here a terrible secret, and someone will kill me if he knows I have it."

Angus stared at the shopping bag.

"It's not really from Harrod's," she explained with a proud note in her voice. "I was just pretending."

Well, diddle a Doberman, he thought; right here in front of him was what he had been dispatched to find. Cradled in the arms of the woman he now loved. He wished the padre of his old regiment were here as well, to help him sort out the predicament of paid employment versus the dictates of his crusty old heart.

If he betrayed Milo Yonker and Claudius Cana, his life wouldn't be worth a farthing; if he betrayed Lizzy Howgath, his life wouldn't be worth living.

"Son of a bitch," he whispered.

"Clever, wasn't it," she answered.

The bloody twinkle was back.

He cleared his throat. "Lizzy," he said solemnly, "what had you intended to do with this . . . secret of yours?"

She blinked prettily. "Why, turn it over to the only man who can stop Merkleton from becoming a graveyard."

He stepped back in amazement. "You're joking!"

"No, Angus. I only wish I were."

"But . . . but . . . that's monstrous!"

Tears instantly filled her eyes. "But Angus, I'm only trying to do what's right!"

"No, no," he snapped. "I mean the graveyard part."

"Well, of course it's monstrous," she snapped back. "Why the hell do you think I'm risking life and limb to get this secret to the only man who can save this wonderful village from such a horrid fate?"

Not only spunky but feisty, he thought with blossoming admiration.

She closed the foggy gap between them and looked up into his eyes. "Angus. Angus, will you help me?"

Before he could respond, they were taken by the sound of approaching footsteps. Hasty ones that had Lizzy shifting around nervously to his side, while he surreptitiously bunched his fists in his pockets and peered intently into the fog. Within seconds a roundish purple figure coalesced out of the dark; seconds later a well-fed weasel in a gold-trimmed purple robe strode boldly up to them, tipped back his hood, and said, "Well, this is a surprise, old man."

"Angus?" Lizzy said fearfully.

Angus nodded curtly. "Evening, Milo."

Yonker rubbed his hands together. "I perceive that the woman is wearing a red coat."

"Angus?"

"Got it in one, mate."

"Am I to understand that you have . . . dare I believe that you have succeeded already?"

"Angus!"

Angus merely swallowed.

"Well, then," the weasel said with supreme satisfaction. "What say we finish her now and get it over with?"

Lizzy backed away. "Finish me off?"

Angus narrowed his eyes. "Milo, what're you getting on about?"

Yonker replied by pulling a revolver from his topcoat pocket and aiming it at Lizzy's head. "There's no time left, Angus. I can wait no longer for the prize."

"Oh . . . Angus!"

There was such disappointment, such dismay, such undiluted passion in his name that Angus closed his eyes, prayed that he was about to make the right decision, opened his eyes again, and clubbed Milo Yonker square atop his hood. The man crumpled, and Angus snatched the gun before it touched the ground.

"The man you have to see," he said urgently. "Who is it? Where is he?"

But Lizzy was in mild shock. She could not take her eyes from the gun, his face, the man lying so still on the pavement, and all that activity was clearly making her nauseous.

"Lizzy! C'mon, woman! The name! The place!"

Finally she looked only at him. "I don't know where he is. That's why I was at the pub." She looked at Yonker. "I was told he went there several times a week, when he could." She looked at the gun. "I'm babbling, aren't I?"

Like a bloody parade of ducks, he thought sourly.

"Darling, who . . . is . . . the . . . man?"

"Why, Kent Montana."

Angus grinned. "Well, pardon my French, but holy shit!"

"You know him?"

"No."

Lizzy reeled. "But—"

"—but I know where he is."

"You don't!"

"I do!"

"You can't!"

"The hell you say."

She grabbed his arm beseechingly. "Angus, will you explain this peculiar incident later? Will you exonerate yourself in my eyes so that I'll continue to love you, even though a shadow of suspicion will follow us for the rest of our days and make our life together all that more exciting?''

"If it'll save time, consider it done."

"Oh, thank God!"

And for the first time in a decade, Angus Dean kissed a woman he loved. The others didn't count.

Then he took her arm and led her away.

Back toward Rains Lane.

Into the fog.

Toward the one man his woman claimed could save Merkleton from a fate she didn't deserve.

"For the tenth time, you silly cow, I am *not* a hooker!" declared Hazel Bloodlowe as she hiked up her skirt and fished in her garter belt for her identification.

"Well, you certainly look like one to me," huffed Ethel Queen from her place behind the register. Etta sat on a stool beside her, an ice pack strapped to her head. "And stop doing things like that in public!"

"I'm getting my goddamn badge," Hazel snarled.

The hidden bulldog growled.

"Here, language, young lady!"

"Sod the language," Hazel muttered, and when she finally found the badge, she held it up, smiled triumphantly, and said, "So tell me again what happened."

Etta moaned and swayed.

Ethel blushed and said, "Oh my, we daren't."

"But if you saw what you said you saw, even though I didn't see it myself, surely you'll want to report it. Otherwise, how will anybody know that you saw it?"

"I don't want folks thinking me daft."

"Who's going to know?"

"You will."

"Well, I'm not going to say anything, I promise you. They'll think I'm nuts."

"There, you see?"

Hazel took a deep breath.

From somewhere behind the counter Archie slobbered.

"But really," she said in her best humor-the-nutter voice. "Think about it—how can you expect me to believe that some-

one snuck in here while you were standing right at the door,
trashed your shop, and then . . . then . . . ''

"See?" Ethel said smugly. "You can't even say it yourself,
can you?"

Etta moaned.

"And," continued Ethel, "if a hooker can't say it, how do
you expect a decent woman such as meself to?"

"I am *not* a hooker. I just look like one."

"You got that right," Etta managed.

Hazel glared, looked around the shop, and said, "That's it,
then. I give up. If you change your mind, call the station,
someone will take your complaint." She headed for the door.
"But for god's sake, don't mention my name."

"All well and good for you to say, isn't it," Etta snapped
heatedly as she readjusted the ice pack and kicked out at the
bulldog. "You weren't the one what saw what I saw, were
you, dearie? You weren't there to see an invisible man show
his privates right in my very own shop that I own with my best
friend. No, no, you weren't. So don't you go all high and
mighty on me, you tart. You just tell them what was here, and
tell them I said I ain't no loony."

Hazel examined the fog for some time before looking over
her shoulder. "If the bloke was invisible, Miss Queen, how
could you see his privates?"

Ethel gasped.

Etta rolled up her sleeves, rolled them down again, and said
in a quiet voice, "I don't know. Why don't you ask him? He's
standing right behind you."

For all its nonpalatial faults, Kent truly enjoyed staying at
the Bowlingham.

The pre-Ringstone hostelry was neither pretentious nor expensive, neither a lure for the boisterous young nor a settling
ground for pensioners waddling out for another last fling in the
big city before they chucked it.

To the left of the entrance—several sets of double glass
doors beneath a square marquee with the hotel's name in tasteful orange neon—were two coffin-size elevators and the porter's desk; to the right was registration. The lobby itself was
deep, marble-pillared, with a jungle of high-backed couches
and armchairs set in convivial squares through which one made
one's way to either the restaurant or the bar.

A haven; a sanctuary; a place his mother wouldn't be caught dead in, much to his chagrin.

Thus had he become known to all the staff, and thus did the staff on duty that night not turn a single hair or jaundiced eye as he made his way nonchalantly through the empty lobby with a hooker on one arm. At least, they acknowledged among themselves, he didn't strike immediately for the elevator, which was so small as to have forced a conclusion of his lordship's business long before he reached the top floor.

The residents' bar, to which the couple repaired, was tucked into the rear righthand corner of the lobby and separated from it by a pinewood and glass wall. Inside were cozy couches, cozy chairs, cozy wall-benches with curved upholstered arms to make cozy conversational islets, square wood pillars for the drunks to use to find the door, and the bar itself, which would have been cozy as well had it not been so crowded with middle-aged and elderly men trying to get their drinks and pick up one of the bartenders, one of either sex, though the men didn't seem to discriminate.

Janice eyed the whole thing suspiciously.

Kent led her to an unused corner, settled her on a tiny couch, and fetched several drinks apiece on a rather large tray, since it was clear that many of those at the bar had been trying to get served since the last election.

His was lager; hers were double scotches.

Once done, he sat opposite her across a small table, shrugged off his jacket, sighed, and decided not to kick off his shoes; she, on the other hand, did kick off her shoes, then took off her coat and reached back to unpin her hair, which prompted a retired colonel at the next table to pop his monocle and grunt a lot.

Kent didn't blame him.

In his entire professional and private life, he had never seen a woman like this. Take away all that heavy-duty makeup and that garish clothing, and she was downright pleasant on the eyes. Pert English nose, delightful apple-cheeks, teasing dimpled chin, bowed red lips, and a lace-and-ruffled blouse that simply cried out for a size or two larger, the crying being done solely by the puritans and liberationists hovering in the background. Easy now, he cautioned; easy, boy, you're in danger, this is business.

Though he did cast a rueful glance at the elevators when she plucked the blouse daintily away from her chest.

Janice, in the meantime, drank one of her doubles in two gulps, the second in three, and held the third between her hands while her eyes watered and her lips quivered.

He waited.

She hiccupped, settled herself with a sigh, and said, "Just so you know, I am not a hooker."

He nodded. "You're the police."

"How . . . how did you know?"

"I saw you flash a badge at poor Flora last night."

"Oh dear. I had hoped I was being discreet." She sighed again, and he wished she would stop doing that. If nothing else, it would keep his mind on the situation and the colonel's monocle from being wedged into the wrong eye. "Hard to be, in these clothes. Discreet, I mean. Not a hooker. That part was easy."

He cocked an eyebrow. "Really?"

"It's my job. Police, I mean. Not a hooker. Being one and being one aren't the same, you see."

"No, I suppose not."

"So who hit you, m'lord?" she asked in husky innocence.

"Kent," he corrected hastily. "Call me Kent. That's my professional name, but it'll do for the moment. The only time I trade on my baronage is when I try to have my mother beheaded. I'm still trying to work it out."

She frowned, let it pass. "So who hit you?"

He sipped at his drink and stared at the wall behind her, not sure why he hesitated. But trusting his instincts, he smiled instead and said, "I believe, Miss Plase—"

"Detective Constable."

"—that, if I have these things right, this is the point in our early relationship where I ask you what, exactly, brought you to Rains Lane on this particular evening two nights in a row, and why you are so curiously interested in my story that you followed me into a killer fog, dangerous though it must have been for you, and allowed me, a total baronial stranger, to pick you up." He frowned, counted on his fingers, wrinkled his nose. "Yes, I think that's right."

"It is?" she said, wide-eyed.

"I think so. Did I miss something?"

"No. That is, yes. But you said dangerous. That part. It was?"

He felt his smile grow slightly waxen. "Detective Constable Plase, an unknown intruder sneaks into my favorite pub, tries several times to bash my head in with a steel pipe, nearly breaks the shoulder of another man, then escapes unseen into the fog where he could have been waiting to try again, as you must have known, and you don't call that dangerous?" Candid admiration pursed his lips. "If I may be so bold—you are quite something else, as the Americans say."

"He was?"

"Was what?"

"Waiting? Out there?" She pointed a trembling finger. "In the fog?"

"Well, surely you must have assumed that."

"Oh dear," she said.

Oh boy, he thought.

She tilted her head back and drank.

The colonel stumbled out of his chair and zigzagged toward the bar.

"Excuse me," Kent said quietly when she reached for yet another glass and emptied it without a whimper, "but I thought you wanted to know who hit me?"

Her violet eyes blinked so rapidly, his hair blew nearly back off his forehead. "Hit you?"

He drank. He wiped his eyes. He said, "Janice—if I may; it's not quite so formal—how long, exactly, have you been a Detective Constable?"

She looked at her watch.

"Never mind," he said.

She lowered her arm and smiled gamely. "I'm sorry. I'm not terribly good at this, am I? If Hazel were here—"

"Hazel?"

"The other hooker."

"Ah."

"Anyway, she's much better. It's her temperament, I expect. She would persist until she either had an answer or had browbeaten you into submission." She fumbled in her handbag, yanked out a compact, and looked at herself in the mirror. "Jesus, I look like a hooker!"

"I don't know."

"What? You think I dress like this all the time?" She half rose from her seat in indignation. "You think I enjoy tarting up and laying myself bare for miserable eyes like yours to feed on me like sharks that can't wait to undress an easy porpoise?''

The colonel returned, choked, and left again.

Kent leaned over the table and grabbed her wrist until she stopped glowering, flushing, and panting. ''No,'' he said calmly. ''What I meant was, I don't know who hit me. Zero says he saw him, but Zero's blind.'' He chuckled. ''He claims that the man was invisible.''

''Oh lord,'' Janice whispered.

Oops, he thought, I think she believes it.

''I didn't see him either,'' she confessed.

Hell.

''So. What do we do now?'' he asked, so close to her that their noses almost touched.

''You could lick my nose,'' she said dreamily.

''I could get arrested.''

A throat was cleared.

Kent rolled his eyes and leaned back, his head bouncing off the colonel's paunch.

''Pardon me,'' the man said, ''but I believe that your friend here has a friend out there who is looking for her.'' He turned and pointed dramatically at the glass and wood partition, through which they could all see Hazel Bloodlowe weaving hysterically through the lobby furniture. ''If she ever sobers up, have her sent to my room.'' And he returned to his seat, where he promptly fell into a deep study of the foam in his mug.

''Stay,'' Kent told Janice, and hurried out of the bar, just in time to catch Hazel before the night porter caught her. ''I'm Kent Montana,'' he said, hustling her toward the entrance. ''Janice is with me.''

She only nodded mutely, and he was acutely aware that she was trembling as if she'd just dashed naked through a blizzard, an image which, while not as dramatic as the other one, was certainly more palatable. On the whole, however, he preferred Janice Plase, who gave her partner the spare drink, sent Kent to fetch others, and chafed the woman's hands until she was able to indicate with a final loud gasp that she was at last under control.

''You will never guess in a million years what I just saw,'' she said.

Janice and Kent shrugged simultaneously.

''An invisible man!''

"Have a drink," Janice suggested.

Kent, however, stayed the hand that lifted the offered glass. "How invisible was he?"

"Not completely."

"I see." He looked at Janice. "Sounds like the man who attacked me, doesn't it?"

"Oh my god," she said.

"Ladies," he said after a moment's contemplation, "I think we are all either too drunk to know what we're saying, much less what we've seen, or we have a serious problem."

Hazel fluffed her hair. "I haven't had a drink all night."

Janice said, "He wants to lick my nose."

And Kent pushed himself to his feet, walked steadily through the bar to the lobby, and stood with hands in his pockets at the hotel entrance.

Watching the fog.

~III~

The Secret

• 1 •

Above the King's Hump, the front room, with attached bath and exorbitant rates, was unlit save for a feeble glow from a streetlamp up the road.

It didn't matter.

He didn't need a lamp or a match to find his way around. Everything was as it had been when he'd moved in and had carefully arranged the equipment to his liking. He could have walked through the place blindfolded and never once spilled a drop of the chemicals, bumped into the burners, or barked his shins on the feeble furniture. In fact, he had done so only the other day, just to prove to himself that his senses were still intact, that his mind was still sharp, that his ability to learn was as remarkable as ever.

All of which made his failure all the more frustrating.

He stood now at the window that overlooked the Lane, hands clasped before him, gaze on the clouds of fog that teased the hour past midnight.

He was tired.

Very tired.

If he didn't pace himself properly, he would collapse from exhaustion, and then where would he be?

Too easy by half, he told himself sourly.

He would be back in Y——, that's where he'd be. Back at the heatless, draughty, deserted farmhouse, back at the inadequate but sufficient library, back at the very beginning of his tortuous journey into and out of Hell.

No. He could not go through all that again. He had to rest. He had to regroup. He had to waken in the morning with fresh body and fresh mind, ready to tackle the insurmountable and mold it to his will.

Of course, he thought as he turned away from the city that had spurned him so long ago, he could always go out and kill someone. That too would be invigorating.

But not yet.

Soon.

The test run tonight had admittedly been a good one, especially the playlet with that simpering flower girl. But it had not been perfect by any means or measure; encouraging, yes, but not conclusive, despite the setback, despite the fact that he had learned, too late, that his coincidental victim had been, coincidentally, the one man he had vowed to destroy above all others.

No, he told himself sternly, there was still a good deal of work to be done, and then . . . then . . . *then* would he unleash the scourge upon the streets that had once been his for the asking.

The Red Moon Festival would no longer be a fond memory for tourists and locals alike; it would instead be the starting line for a lifelong race through nightmares, terror, and the judgment of death.

Slowly he made his way across the thin-carpeted floorboards to the marble-framed fireplace, where low flames burned between two blackened andirons. He used a sooty poker to stoke the ashes and embers, dropped on two more puny logs, then sat on a low stool and held out his hands to warm them. Behind him, on a scarred wood table nearly as long as the room itself, casting their writhing shadows against the opposite wall, was an ominous array of bubbling beakers and ocher test tubes, petri dishes and microscopes and mortars and pestles and all kinds of things he didn't have names for but had seemed useful at the time he robbed the chemist's shop in Birmingham and the pharmaceutical warehouse outside Coventry.

It didn't matter, though, if he knew the proper names or not.

What mattered was what he had done with the equipment.

He smiled.

He chuckled.

"Fools," he whispered. "All of them, fools."

Feeling his pulse begin to rise, his cheeks flush, he reached around the corner of the fireplace and pulled into his lap a battered guitar.

A slow strum to assure that it was still in tune.

"Fools."

A clearing of his throat and a swift attack of the scales, an arpeggio all the more dazzling because no fingers were to be seen plucking the strings or covering the frets.

"Fools!" he shouted. "Fools, to think that you have bested me!"

He tilted back his head and laughed, laughed until his chest hurt, laughed until the cats in the alley ran for their masters, rats in the alley ran for their nests, drunks in the alley ran for their lives.

A pealing, maniacal, triumphant laugh.

That soon dissolved into the words of a ballad he had written a score of years ago, about a fast-loving railroad man and his sweetheart and the tough but tender life they'd led until his death in a collision at Waterloo Station.

Their poignancy had once made him a star; now they only made him angry.

And when the last line faded into the fading embers on the hearth, when the slow-spoken, emotion-fraught words *"Though he's my Brit Rail baby, he always comes too late"* drifted forlornly into the wormy woodwork, Racig Dargren placed the guitar between his invisible knees, closed his eyes, and lowered his head to the silent cheers and the silent wild applause.

A log split; sparks spiraled up the chimney.

A gust of wind rattled the panes.

He opened his eyes and stared at his left foot.

A twitch of his lips.

A glance at his crotch, now mercifully lost to ordinary sight.

A check of the foot again, clear as the bell upon which he wanted to bang his head.

"Well, shit," he said, and hoped that he'd remembered his socks.

~IV~

The Terror

◆ 1 ◆

"It seems pretty clear to me," said Kent Montana, who wasn't exactly sure that he knew what he was about to talk about, "that we're faced with a scientific phenomenon which, under ordinary circumstances, would probably be considered impossible."

Janice mumbled, then groaned.

He didn't blame her; he wasn't feeling all that well himself and, since it wasn't yet noon, he was more than a little tempted to crawl back into bed and forget the whole damn thing.

There were, unfortunately, the lumps on his head.

He persevered.

"But since we have the testimony of a trained observer—your colleague in arms, Hazel—and the puzzling evidence of my own friend, Zero, even if he is blind, I don't think we can discount it entirely."

She mumbled again, and gurgled a bit too.

Under ordinary conditions, he would have required something a bit more intelligible in the way of professional police feedback; however, unless his mother had miraculously become extraordinarily creative, these were no ordinary conditions.

He persevered.

"Unfortunately, because of this seeming paradox—an invisible man who isn't quite entirely invisible to those who claim to have seen him—neither do I think we can safely go to your superiors at this time and tell them what we know. Quite frankly they'd probably laugh us into the street."

He squirmed around in his chair and looked across the room, through the open bathroom door. The detective constable stood rigidly at the basin, wrapped from neck to intriguing bare ankle in his favorite robe, brushing her teeth with an index finger while her free hand splayed over the mirror, covering her reflection.

''But now that it's daylight,'' he continued, ''I think we're in pretty good shape.''

She turned her head and stared.

He sighed and turned away. He himself was at the desk with the attached blow dryer, over which was another mirror that told him, without pulling any punches, that another night sacked out on the floor was going to permanently dent both cheeks, his brow, and one of his ears. He looked like hell. He felt like hell. The window, not a foot from his right elbow, told him it was hell outside, too—more rain than he had seen in a year, all coming down at once.

And not a single word from his agent about his next project.

Life, he thought, can be so complicated sometimes.

He shifted the chair; the bathroom jerked into view. Another shift, and he could see Janice desperately trying to rinse out her mouth without running the water much louder than a trickle.

He glanced at the rumpled bed and sighed; he glared at the carpeted floor and sneered.

The previous evening had finally ended with the closing of the bar and the two undercover constables deciding that, whether they were drunk or not, something peculiar aside from all the Druids was going on in Merkleton, and Kent Montana seemed to be part of it. Unless, of course, he was a completely innocent victim of random violence, in which case there was nothing to worry about at all because they were, then, drunk and there was no invisible creature, man or otherwise. However, just to be on the safe side, they proceeded to divide between them the burdens of the rest of the night in order to ensure that his lordship survive until morning without the threat of further assault.

He had not protested.

Hazel had chosen to remain in the lobby with Reg Olifer, the night porter, the better to make sure that neither elevator was utilized by anyone other than the hotel's legal patrons; Janice had thus, by default, been elected to guard him in his room, which she had done rather well for a good five minutes before passing out on the bed.

Propriety had put Kent on the floor with his topcoat for a pillow.

And kept him there by way of Janice's disturbing tendency to lash out with her fists while she slept and snored.

I have been, he admitted as he stared bleakly at the rain, in more romantic situations in my time; though he also admitted to no discernible guilt that he also wished he had been at least semi-conscious when she had, sometime before dawn, tossed off her tart's clothes and chosen his robe for a nightgown.

"You see," he explained to her reflection as she staggered back into the room and dropped onto the mattress, "the man is invisible, but he's not a ghost."

"Yes," she whispered hoarsely.

He smiled. "What I mean is, we can't see him because he's transparent. But he can't walk through walls."

"Clever," she agreed, toppling slowly backward.

Her reflection flashed a bit of knee and shin as the robe slipped apart at the waist.

Propriety forbade him from looking any higher.

Or shifting the chair farther to the right so he wouldn't have to look any higher.

"What that means is, the rain," and he pointed at the window, forgetting how close it was and damn near jamming his finger into his elbow, "will hit him like it hits us, you see? He'll make a path through it. We won't be able to see his features, but we will be able to know where he is. Or isn't. In a manner of speaking."

"Right," she groaned, and idly scratched at a thigh.

Propriety refused to indulge in useless speculation.

"Now all we have to figure out is, who he is, why he's after me, where he's staying, and—"

Her scratching shifted to the flat of her chest, and propriety got stuffed into the desk's top drawer.

As casually as he could, he bumped his chair around until he could face her, stretch out his legs, and prop his stockinged feet on the bed, next to one knee.

The knee shifted.

"Janice," he said sternly, "you're not making this any easier."

She looked blearily at him without raising her head. "If you're thinking what I think you're thinking, your lordship, then you must be a necrophiliac." A palm floated to her forehead. Her other hand kept scratching. "And it seems to me that he must be staying somewhere around here."

He crossed his legs, they fell from the mattress, he shifted the chair closer and lifted them again. "How do you reckon that?"

"He was naked."

"He's invisible."

"Naked, invisible, it's still bloody cold and wet out there, and if I were him, I wouldn't be wandering too far from home. I'd catch pneumonia. And then where would I be? How could I do whatever horrid thing it is I'm going to do if I have pneumonia and keep sneezing all the time? Speaking of which, I think I'm dying."

He smiled. "You don't drink much, do you?"

Her own lips managed a smile of their own. "You noticed that, did you?"

He waggled a hand side to side.

"I don't eat much either, it seems," she complained. "You feel we might have some breakfast, m'lord?"

"Kent."

"Feed me."

Noting that his own stomach bubbled in sudden anticipation, he stood, bewailed the stiffness that ranged along the left side of his floor-battered body, and opened the wardrobe, ducked under the attached television set, and clucked at the clothes neatly placed therein. Finally, after desultory deliberation, he tossed slacks and a sweater over his head. "Try these on. Roll up the legs. They'll have to do until we can get you something else."

"But—"

"You want to look like a hooker in broad daylight?"

Seconds later, much to his chagrin and with considerable damage to his ego, she was in the bathroom, the door closed; seconds after that, himself in jeans, shirt, and light sweater with matching jacket, they were in the elevator.

"Kent?"

He stared at the numbers winking down to the lobby from the top floor.

"Why are you so calm about this? If it were I being possibly pursued by an invisible killer, I would be hysterical. I mean, it stands to reason, doesn't it?"

The elevator jounced at the bottom.

Janice grabbed his arm and groaned.

The door opened; he turned to her and said, "It is not my nature to be hysterical, Detective Constable Plase. It is my nature to stay alive. Hysterical will come if I have to sleep on the goddamn floor again."

He turned around, and a corpse swayed before them.

"Jesus Christ!" he shouted.

Janice grabbed his arm and nearly yanked it from its socket.

The corpse belched.

Kent slapped at his chest to get his lungs working again. "Good Lord, Colonel," he said, sidling uneasily into the lobby, "you look like hell."

The retired colonel saluted smartly, looked at Janice, and said, "Get her some decent clothes and send her up to my room," before falling into the car, the door mercifully closing behind him.

"Who . . . ?"

He spotted Hazel's fur coat carelessly tossed over the night porter's desk. "Colonel Lumet Braithe. Retired. He owns the place." He leaned over the porter's station, grabbed an umbrella, and looked to his right, to the cloakroom door.

It was closed.

No, he thought charitably; give the woman some credit. She's probably nipped out for coffee or something.

Janice tapped his shoulder. "Do you think we could—"

Someone coughed politely.

Kent swung toward the entrance, frowned when he saw no one, then glanced down. At a man. A man wearing a tailored grey trench-coat with matching muffler, a nondescript grey hat, and black galoshes whose silver buckles chinked when his foot shifted.

"Oh lord," Kent muttered.

The man was kneeling, his arms stretched out behind him.

Dear god, Kent thought.

"If I may have a minute, your lordship?" the man said to the carpeting.

Flying steel pipes, sort of invisible men, a cop who wants me to lick her nose, and now this.

Inspector Herman Easewater, of the Merkleton constabulary.

"For god's sake, Herman," Kent whispered loudly, glancing around the lobby in hopes that none of the hotel's residents were witness to this display.

The inspector rose. High. Very high. He was at least six inches taller than Kent, a good hundred muscular pounds heavier, and a fair decade older. His nonetheless youthful face was pleasantly round, his cheeks a cheery autumnal red, and his jaw and chin covered by a meticulously trimmed dark brown beard. He smiled self-consciously and swept off his hat, which sprayed Kent with rainwater.

"Oh my god!" Easewater gasped in shock, and yanked a sponge from his trench-coat pocket. Before Kent could protest, the policeman proceeded to daub at the offending droplets, moving his way swiftly down Kent's jeans to his boots until he was kneeling again.

"Oh my *god!*" the man gasped again. He looked up, awe infusing his reddening features. "These . . ." He pointed to the boots. "I recognize these!"

Kent didn't know whether to laugh or put a knee in the man's chin.

"You . . . my heavens, I recognize this slice, your lordship," he said with barely restrained excitement, pointing a trembling finger at an imperfection on the left toe. "You wore these very same boots in the episode when you discovered that the cook was having an affair with the gardener's daughter, just after your late mistress was found strangled in the conservatory by the trollop who lived above the Chinese restaurant, herself the unknown daughter of the chauffeur who was the gardener's brother once removed." He touched the toe reverently. "I never thought I'd live to see the day."

My sentiments exactly, Kent thought.

"Inspector."

Easewater looked up, blinked, suddenly realized his position, and stood with a haste that nearly broke Kent's neck as he tried to maintain eye contact. "Most sorry, m'lord." He replaced his hat. "Terribly sorry." He pulled out a clear-plastic evidence bag from a pocket, gingerly placed the sponge therein, and tucked it away. "My fault." He jammed his hands into his pockets and shrugged. "Frightfully sorry."

"It's all right, Herman." Kent smiled. "And what brings you out on a morning like this? Druids rob the bank or something? Claudius run off with the Festival funds?"

The inspector seemed ill at ease. "Well, sir, it's like this, sir—there was a bit of a do the last two nights at the King's Hump, as I'm sure you remember."

"You can say that again," he said, and looked over at Janice, who wasn't there. Anywhere. He frowned.

"Ordinarily," Easewater continued, "I wouldn't be concerned, so to speak, except that I subsequently learned that you, sir, were involved as a victim, so to speak. Both times, in fact."

He took off his hat, carefully. "As you are who you are, sir, quite naturally I took it upon myself to make sure there were no suspicious circumstances surrounding the circumstances."

Kent's frown rearranged itself into a frown of an entirely different interpretation. "Suspicious circumstances, Inspector?"

"Possible assassin, sir. Being a peer of the realm and all. You, that is, sir. M'lord. Sir."

"Ah."

Easewater nodded sagely. "So, if you don't mind a few questions, m'lord, I'll have my man assist you with the statement. Just for the record, so to speak. So—" He stopped, scowled, and turned to the glass-front entrance. Outside, a police constable stood with hands behind his back. Easewater whistled sharply, the constable turned, saw the inspector, saw Kent, and raced inside as best he could through the revolving doors.

You'll be all right, Kent assured himself; it could be worse.

Police Constable Ralph Geeter was, charitably, ancient. If the Empire was older, it was only by a few seconds. The only reason Kent could figure why the man was still in uniform was that Geeter was the sole member of the Merkleton force who could take on-the-spot notes in shorthand without having to ask afterward what the squiggle with the loop meant.

PC Geeter saluted the inspector, bowed to Kent, popped a spiral notepad from his tunic pocket, and snapped a pen from behind his pebbled ear.

Easewater cleared his throat. "Your lordship, is there anything about last night which you care to add to the official report?"

Kent shrugged.

"Right, then. Constable!"

PC Geeter snapped his notepad shut, replaced the pen, saluted the inspector, bowed to Kent, and quick-marched back outside to glare at the pedestrians.

Inspector Easewater put on his hat and trimmed the brim. "So sorry, m'lord, for bothering you. The tourists, you see. Can't have them getting the wind up about a brawl. Bad for business, you understand. Especially as we're coming to the Festival finale and all. Don't want panic in the streets, now do we?"

"Of course not, Herman. Glad to be of assistance."

Easewater saluted, apologized for disturbing his lordship, and backed out to the street through the revolving door, which confused the hell out of him. Seconds later, he and the constable marched off into the rain.

A loud sigh for having escaped close questioning, and thus possibly revealing either the terror of a truly invisible man or a night of supreme drunkenness, and Kent turned abruptly, immediately collided with Janice, who grinned up at him.

"Problem?" she asked.

"Where the hell were you?"

She took his arm, snuggled against it, winked at him, and said, "A private matter. Feed me, Baron." Then she looked down at her bare feet. "No, clothe me first. Then feed me. Then we'll see what we can do about solving all your troubles."

It was then, as they stepped outside, that he began to suspect that this woman with a grip of newly forged iron was not at all what she seemed, even with no shoes on. Surely, were she what she claimed to be, she would have had to report to the station by now, or at least stuck around to report to Easewater, who was, after all, her detective superior. Surely, were she truly an undercover detective constable on a mission, there would be a second professional team poised and ready to take over for the daylight hours. Surely, if she were a policewoman in the truest sense, she'd not waste time buying clothes and stuffing her mouth at his expense, but would be out on the street, diligently hunting down clues, ruthlessly interrogating suspects, and flashing her badge left and right to intimidate the populace into volunteering its cooperation.

Surely.

Of course, it *was* raining like a sonofabitch.

But surely—

Thunder exploded over Merkleton.

The storm intensified.

Daylight became twilight.

And Kent Montana realized that, in spite of his bravado and clever expostulation of the facts as he knew them, he was not only getting drenched because she was holding the umbrella, but he was also feeling not unlike a helpless puppet manipulated by hidden strings.

He didn't like either feeling.

Something would have to be done.

·2·

"Lord, I'm so sorry!" Lizzy Howgath wailed piteously. "I don't know what happened. I'm so miserable I could just die."

"Not to worry, love," Angus said soothingly. "Not to worry. We just got turned around in the fog, that's all. Nothing to fear, you'll see." He patted her arm gently. "All we need to do now is find a cab. He'll take us to this man straight away."

"Do you think so?"

"I'm sure of it."

"I'm just so . . . so . . . confused!"

"Well, I'm bound to admit, this certainly doesn't look like the Merkleton I used to know."

"Not with all those cows, no."

"On the other hand—"

"Darling, be straight with me—are we lost?"

"No. We just don't know where we are."

"Angus, you must know so much to be able to make such fine distinctions!"

"Not as much as would get us back. I'm a proper failure as a sailor, ain't I?"

"Well, it's not your fault you're not really a sailor."

"True enough."

"So let's just find a likely place for cabs. Once we do that, there'll be no stopping us. Unless . . ."

"Yes?"

"That man. Last night? Suppose he finds us again?"

"Not to worry. I think, just now, he has bigger problems."

"Did you . . . kill him?"

"No. But if I ever see him again, he'll wish I had."

86

"Such a temper, Angus Dean."

"My curse, Lizzy. I admit it."

"And such rain! Do you think it will ever stop?"

"Eventually."

"And such a comfort. Why, Angus, if we weren't smack in the middle of some street or other, I just might do something to embarrass us both horribly."

"Oh, Lizzy, if you only—"

"Angus!"

"Jesus Christ, what?"

"A cab!"

Claudius Cana stood at the door of his exclusive tailor shop, diagonally across the High Street from the park entrance, and watched the rain without noticeable expression. His left hand idly brushed at the lapels of his self-tailored velvet tuxedo; his right hand held the wolf's-head cane and thumped it monotonously against the floor.

He sniffed.

He cleared his throat.

He did his best not to count the money all the merchants and entrepreneurs were losing, his cut of which would have kept him in wool and satin for months if he weren't going to conquer the world when this was all over.

Which reminded him: "Poetra, my darling?"

Poetra Pioll, perched on a walnut-trimmed display case of paisley ties, crossed her legs and flicked a cigarette ash on the floor. "Yes, darling?"

"My man has not fingered the woman yet."

"I should hope not."

His smile was brittle. "Poetra, please."

"I'm sorry, Claudius. It's all this rain. It depresses me."

"And me as well, my love. And me." He turned his bulk and adjusted his scarf. "The rain, we are told, will clear up in an hour or so. Business as usual on the Green. But I must have what I must have before the sacrificial pageant!" The cane stabbed the floor. "There is no time to waste."

Poetra agreed. "Do you think perhaps your man has gone into business for himself?"

"Bah! He is too stupid for that. Ex-army, you know. Not an independent thought in his entire head."

"But the woman," she suggested suggestively. "Might he be turned by the woman?"

"Gads! I never thought of that."

Poetra slid off the display case and hobbled on her spike heels over to him. "Darling," she said, adjusting his tie, "if you're going to run the world, you'll have to think of things like that."

"I suppose so. But damn!"

A hand patted his shoulder. "Now, Claudius, control yourself. We must have clear heads, right? Can't run things without a clear head." She cocked a hip. "So. Do you suppose that our man—not the hired man, but the other one—do you suppose that he might come to the Festival himself?"

Claudius blinked.

He hadn't thought of that.

"My God!" A sort of a smile twitched his pudgy lips. "You know, that's entirely possible. In fact—" He clapped his hands, once, sharply. "In fact, if he suspected that the Howgath woman was here, he . . ." He giggled. "Lord, he just might come back. He just might come back to take back what is rightfully his!" He laughed.

"Pretty farfetched, if you ask me," she said. "I'm hungry, Claudius. Can't we get an early lunch, please?"

But Claudius whipped around as best he could to face the High Street again. This was perfect. This was magnificent. If the zombie was right, he could take possession of the notebooks that stupid woman carried, and in the bargain, kill the one man who might cause him problems in a legal sense.

Oh Lord, he thought, this is indeed a grand day!

Then he frowned.

It was bad enough having to look for a woman in an abominable red coat; how did one look for a man Claudius hadn't seen in over a dozen years?

"Claudius?"

He shook himself and smiled over his shoulder at the one woman dumb enough to stick by him all this time. "Yes, my sweet?"

"I was thinking."

The smile held.

"If you want to find that singer person, maybe we ought to go to that horrid little pub where he used to sing for his supper, or something dreadful like that. If he's been there, maybe someone saw him, and maybe that someone could tell us where he went, or where he might be.''

"And how," he asked calmly, "will we explain ourselves?" He stared pointedly at her elaborately simple evening gown, then down at his tuxedo.

She shrugged. "It's raining. We were on our way home from the theater and we got lost."

"It's not quite noon, yes? And besides, there is no theater in this . . . never mind. Continue."

"Darling, this is terribly boring."

He persisted. "And?"

"Well, how should I know?" she whined in that delightfully submissive way of hers. She took a deep breath. "We pretend to be a little tipsy and start singing one of . . . his . . . things. Some disgusting little man will say, 'Oy, that bloke was just in 'ere, 'e was. Close t'me as I am t'you.' And you, darling, will say, 'Fancy that. Is he here now? I should like to get his autograph.' " She puffed on her holder. "I guess. What do you think?"

He grinned. "I could kiss you, Poetra!"

"My lipstick, Claudius!"

"Figuratively speaking, my love."

"Later. First let's get this over with so I can eat. I'm absolutely starving."

Never again will you hunger, he vowed silently as she took his arm; if this works, I will feed you personally. Anything you want. Anytime you wish.

He paused as he opened the shop door.

"Poetra, I hesitate to ask, but suppose we find nothing?"

"Oh, I don't know. Golly, Claudius, you're the brain around here." She wrinkled her nose, licked her lips, kicked at a cat trying to sneak inside between them. "Go find that dreadful Montana person and torture him until he tells us, I guess."

He laughed. The world was his kingdom, and he had his own personal jester.

Poetra pouted.

"I'm sorry, darling," he wheezed. "But what does Kent Montana have to do with this?"

"Well, you brought him up the other day."

"Just in a manner of speaking, my dear. Just in a manner of speaking." Impulsively he hugged her. "It was merely a test. A jest."

"It was cruel, Claudius."

"Thank you."

She tugged at his arm. "Shall we? We're wasting time."

Racig Dargren, the Welsh Vagabond, knew that he ought to have a spot of lunch before he grew too weak to function.

But he knew as well that he didn't have much time.

Tonight was the sacrifice.

Tonight he would—

He chuckled madly.

He held the beaker up to his eyes, grinned at the gelid, bubbling formula inside, and very carefully placed it on the laboratory table he'd managed to sneak in without that bitch of a landlady noticing. Fastidiously he wiped his hands on a tea towel, picked up a syringe, and filled it with a careful measure of the heated liquid. He had no idea what color it was because of all the green and red atmospheric lights affixed to the room's corners and baseboards, but he didn't complain. Color didn't matter; results did.

A deep breath, a brief prayer for the nonstop work he'd been doing since midnight, and he walked to the wood valet set in front of the window. Draped over its ersatz shoulders was a dark brown jacket. Dargren stroked the material lovingly, pinched the leather elbow patches, sighed when he traced the constellations of glitter and glass studs sewn into the double-width lapels and across the back.

Memories.

Ah, memories.

Then, with a grunt of determination, he injected the formula into the black velvet collar.

Five minutes passed.

Thunder boomed over the pub and trembled the window.

"*I will climb Nelson's column, I will swim the River Thames*," he sang softly to himself, keeping time with his left foot.

Six minutes.

"*I will walk the moors in the bright full moon*."

Seven minutes.

The rain hardened.

"*If only you'll be my friend*."

Eight minutes.

His left foot faded.

"*Baby.*"

The brown jacket didn't.

He cackled.

He chortled.

In the rain-streaked window he could see the ghostly reflection of his teeth.

The jacket remained the same.

He exploded with laughter, abruptly wept in frustration, suddenly whirled and threw the syringe into the mouth of the fireplace.

"Damn!" he screamed, his fists raised to the tumultuous heavens. "Damn you! Damn you!"

Then, with a choking sob, he realized he had just destroyed his last means of subdural injection. He glared. He threw a glass. He threw a chair. He stomped over to the closet, threw open the door, and hoped he had enough elastic bandages left to do the job; getting to the chemist's in this weather was going to be a bitch.

"That tears it!" the barman exclaimed, and slapped his towel down on the counter. "That bloody does it!"

"Oh, leave him be, Eddie," Flora said. "He's just having a bad time is all."

They faced each other behind the bar, hands on hips, matching scowl for scowl.

"A bad time, is it?" he sneered. "Well, what about them?"

He gestured in angry frustration at the handful of early luncheon customers, all of whom had stopped in varying stages of eating, forking, slurping, and chewing, and were as one staring apprehensively at the ceiling.

"They'll get over it," she said.

"Well, I won't. Not anymore."

He brushed by her, lifted the counter flap, and stepped through before she could stop him.

"Don't," she begged. "Eddie, please!"

He ignored her. He stamped to the side door, yanked it open, and staggered back with a startled oath when a man pushed through and shoved him aside. He was dressed in a high-collared black topcoat, wide-brimmed black hat, high-topped black boots, wraparound black sunglasses with the price tag still on, and the most amazing array of ugly elastic bandages anyone there could remember.

"Mr. Smith," the barman sputtered.

"Going out," came the muffled reply. "See that I have my lunch tray when I return."

No one spoke as Mr. Smith strode quickly from the pub.

Thunder boomed.

There was a rush for the bar.

"Cor," said the blind man in something akin to awe as he reseated himself by the doorway where he had taken up whistling until his accordion was repaired, "that bloke's got the damnedest teeth I ever saw in my life!"

"You're blind, Zero," Flora growled.

"Right. But it's awful damn funny a bloke's got teeth what don't got no gums."

"Etta," said Ethel Queen from behind the register, "I just saw a man walk by."

Etta, who was trying to keep an eye on four scruffy teenagers with pink and blond hair loitering at the magazine rack, snorted. "You always see a man go by. It's the ones what stop you gotta worry about."

"This one had bandages."

"So?"

"And sunglasses."

"So?"

"Etta, it's raining!"

Behind the counter, Archie growled.

Etta glared at it, glared at the teenagers, glared at the rain. "Well, I don't see nothing, do I?"

" 'Cause he's already gone, isn't he?"

Etta said nothing. She lit a cigarette, a habit she had broken twenty years before. But last night . . . She shuddered when she thought of it, shuddered again when she brought back an image of the hooker's face when *she* had seen it, shuddered a third time when a man walked by, all in black except for the bandages and the teeth.

"Ethel," she said weakly, "stay alert. I'm going back for a little lie-down."

"But what about the store? How do I know how much the spinach is?"

"Ask the damn dog," she growled.

The bulldog growled back.

Unless it was Ethel.

• • •

With some trepidation, Eddie followed Mr. Smith up the back staircase, the laden lunch tray in his hands. At the door, Smith fumbled in his pockets for the key, found it, and inserted it in the lock.

"Just leave it on the floor, Mr. Jones," he ordered, voice muffled by the bandages.

Eddie glanced slyly at the stairwell. "I could wait for the tray, Mr. Smith. Save you the bother."

"No bother."

The bolt turned.

"Just leave it."

Eddie took his time bending his knees, cocked his head when Smith opened the door a crack, and gasped when he saw the horrible green and red lights beyond.

The tray slipped through his fingers and banged loudly to the floor.

Instantly Smith grabbed him by the throat and effortlessly yanked him to his feet, pushed him rapidly down the hall until Eddie came up hard against the wall.

"You saw!" Smith hissed.

Eddie shook his head violently. "Nosir! I seen nothing! I swear, I didn't see nothing!"

Smith squeezed, and Eddie could not believe the power of the man's grip.

"Please!" he begged. "Please, sir, I didn't see anything, I swear to God, I didn't see anything, really, honest, Mr. Smith, I didn't see nothing in there at all."

Embarrassingly he began to weep.

Smith, with a contemptuous snort and tilt of his head, threw the barman aside and stalked back to his room. He picked up the tray, stepped over the threshold, looked back over his shoulder, and said, "Come back for this in an hour, you miserable little toad."

And slammed the door behind him.

It took Eddie what seemed like hours to get to his feet, hours more to make his way shakily to the stairs. But by the time he had reached the ground floor, his terror had been replaced by a bitter rage. No man treated Eddie Jones like that, especially one named, ha!, Smith.

No man.

He would pay for this.

He would pay dearly indeed, and then Flora Tatterall would truly know what kind of man she had hired to work so cheaply beside her.

Kent suspected that the rest of his day, and the rest of his life most likely, wasn't going to go his way at all when Janice suggested they encamp in the lobby instead of returning to his room. It would be, she explained as she led him to the farthest couch from the entrance while still being able to see it and the street beyond, much easier to keep watch on those who came in.

Not to mention spotting the culprit.

He knew he probably ought to remind her that they wouldn't be able to see who they were looking for even if he trod on their toes, but since lunch and the brief shopping spree, she had become so animated and cheerful that he didn't have the heart.

Besides, she looked much better now, fed and rested and without gobs of makeup; and in her new plum skirt suit with the bolero jacket and beige silk blouse with tie collar and pearl buttons, she most assuredly did not look anything like any cop he had ever seen.

What the hell.

It might be interesting, as long as he wasn't killed.

So they sat side by side, backs to the wall, and watched.

The rain finally eased, though distant thunder still grumbled to the south.

Snacks were served to the dozens sitting and drying out and smelling like wet wool in the lobby.

They watched.

The afternoon newspapers were delivered by a slightly wan and baggy-eyed Reg Olifer, on duty early for a change, to the dozens sitting and digesting and discreetly belching in the lobby.

They watched.

The fog, thought by all to have been driven off by the storm, returned—first as a faint mist rising from the streets, then as puffs of tiny clouds that drifted past the hotel and soon merged into a shifting, silent grey wall.

The colonel stopped by to complain that no one was going to be able to see damn-all at the sacrifice tonight if the fog didn't lift and the moon didn't come out.

Ten minutes later, the fog lifted, the sun came out, and the lobby emptied as the dozens hurried off to catch the last of the Festival on the Green. Once the concessions had closed, they'd have to come back and change for the sacrifice and concert, but anything, even soggy grass, beat sitting in the lobby of a hotel on a Saturday during the world-famous Merkleton Red Moon Festival.

Kent picked up a discarded newspaper and read through the want ads, hoping to find a secret message from his agent; he glanced occasionally at Janice, whose eyes were narrowed as she studied each face, each gesture, each movement of the lobby's patrons; he counted the holes in the plaster ceiling; he counted the dropped stitches in his sweater; he wondered if Janice had noticed the man with the bandages who went by twice; he pitied poor Mary Shweet, the local poverty-stricken flower girl passing under the marquee with her pathetic basket of drooped blossoms; he reached over and grabbed Janice's hands.

"All right," he said quietly, "I confess. Whatever the hell it is, I did it, okay?"

She blinked at him in incomprehension.

He nodded at the vista spread before them. "This is one of your police techniques, isn't it? Bore the suspect to death and he'll spill his guts to nipping the Crown Jewels."

A smile stopped him; a pat on his thigh woke him up.

"Kent . . . your lordship . . . Kent. I'm only doing my duty, can't you see that?"

"But I thought we'd decided that our man would be easier to spot in the rain because he'd be almost visible."

"It's not raining."

"It was before."

"It was?"

Oh Jesus.

"Yes, Janice."

"I see. Of course. But we were shopping before, weren't we? And then we had lunch in that French place, didn't we? And then we were in here, weren't we? So we couldn't see him, could we?"

"Not unless he wore a disguise," he said grimly.

"A disguise?" She put a hand to her throat.

"Sure. Like wearing clothes and covering up the invisible

bits with something like elastic bandages or cotton puffs or a scarf or something.''

"What disguise?"

"You're not a detective, are you?"

She blanched.

Damn.

"You're a police constable, aren't you?"

She paled.

Shit.

"You and your partner were probably volunteers for a mission of entrapping helpless citizens into the iniquity of prostitution, you were caught up in this mess we're now caught up in, and you were afraid that I, a baron, would have no truck with a mere police constable."

He grinned.

She reached into her handbag and pulled out a flask, uncorked it, stared at him, sipped the contents, corked the flask, and said, "Cop?"

Trusting himself not to go immediately for her throat, he took the flask and set it firmly on the table in front of them. "Janice, I think it's time we were straight with each other, what do you say? Now, you know who I am, and I now know who you are. You know who you're after, and I know . . . what is after me. You know what happened last night, and I had to sleep on the bloody floor. That makes me stiff. That makes me annoyed. And if you don't stop crushing my leg, I'm going to scream bloody murder."

She snapped her hand back. "Sorry," she said contritely. "Reflex."

"I wish."

"And yes, Kent," she said, facing him squarely, shoulders back, chin up, and distractions on the loose, "all you say is true. And you must also realize that you are now bound by the Official Secrets Act not to say a word to anyone about what we have just discussed."

He gaped. He rubbed his bruised leg. He patted his lumpy head. "What discussed?"

Her smile was sad. "Oh, Kent, please keep your mind on what's to hand. If you don't, we're all lost."

"Not all of us," he countered glumly. "Just some of us."

It was then that Hazel Bloodlowe slammed through the revolving glass door, tripped and spun her way across the lobby, and fell into Kent's lap.

The night porter locked himself in the cloakroom.

Kent grabbed what he could to keep Hazel from falling.

She grabbed what she had to, to keep him from grabbing.

Janice glared at them both and said, "What's all this, then?"

"Innocent," he declared.

"Murder," said Hazel. "Sonofabitch, Janice, we've got a goddamn murder."

· 3 ·

Stan Yarkshore's mum didn't raise her only son to be no idiot most of the time. He had been watching the funny-looking bloke with all the horrid bandages come out of and go into that dingy stairwell for several days now, and it hadn't taken his nose long to bet him that something up there would fetch a pretty penny if only he could get his hands on it.

So he waited.

He drank.

He ate.

He used the Gents and began the cycle again.

Once in a while, he'd amuse himself by ducking into the Lane and snatching someone's wallet, pinch a purse, go down to the Green and ruffle a Druid, then come back in and flirt with the ladies, like he did that long-winded brunette in the execrable red coat. Shame about that one. He'd nearly had her shopping bag when the bloody lights had blown out and he'd been caught on the run by a couple of hookers who must have done their training in the army, for god's sake. He'd been lucky to get away alive that time.

He'd been nervous about coming back too, in case someone had pegged him.

But no one had said a word.

And so he sat.

Drank.

Ate.

Was about to use the Gents and start the cycle all over again when the bandage guy came out. There was some sort of minor set-to at the door with the barman, and when Flora took the man by the ears and dragged him squealing back to his post, all hands laughing and cheering, Stan used the distraction to slip into the stairwell.

Up the steps, quiet as a church mouse.

Then, one eye on the door below and a silent prayer to his mum, rest her soul, he slipped out the leather-encased picks his old man had left him on his deathbed and soon made short work of the lock.

Inside, quick as a wink and Bob's your uncle, and he damn near fainted dead away when his eyes got used to all that green and red lighting.

"Cor," he whispered, silently closing the door behind him. He wasn't a religious man, Stan wasn't, but this . . .

It looked like something out of them movies he used to watch as a kid—smoke and bubbles and noises and stuff. A great long table of it. The smell like rhubarb pie gone bad in the summer sun. A fire going in the grate, though the room was already as hot as effing Madrid in August. And a guitar propped against the wall.

He grinned.

The mysterious Mr. Smith had himself, right here in the middle of Merkleton, his very own drug factory. Everything he needed to slip a dream and a nightmare into someone's unsuspecting brain.

Nothing else it could be.

"Jackpot."

Selling to the tourists and Druids whatever he could get his hands on would make tonight's celebration one hell of a thing to remember.

With as much stealth and native cunning as he could muster, he made his cautious way around the room, checking every box, every drawer, behind everything on the mantel, under every bit of furniture; under the table and on it; behind the drapes, under the carpet scorched and blackened; behind the shower curtain in the bathroom, in the toilet tank, in the toilet, in the basin and bathtub drains.

Nothing.

He sniffed each of the beakers and glass jars and colored vials; he raised and lowered the height of the flames on all the burners; he sifted through the fireplace ashes, shook the hell out of the guitar, and had just begun to tap the walls for secret compartments when he heard footsteps outside.

Quickly he ducked into the bathroom and pulled the door to, leaving it open just a little.

An argument.

Crashing and thumping and curses and sneers.

Stan, boy, he said in a fit of apprehension, could be you've strayed just a wee bit from the path your mum chose for you.

Then Smith stepped into the room, a lunch tray balanced on his hands. He kicked the door closed with his heel, set the tray on the lab table, and locked the door. The key he dropped onto the mantel.

Then he took off his hat and sunglasses.

Stan rubbed his eyes.

"Oh . . . God!" Smith exclaimed, cracking his knuckles, scratching his scalp, shaking himself like a dog just in from the rain. He took a small package from his coat pocket and placed it beside the tray, took off the coat and gloves and threw them carelessly into the corner.

Stan swallowed a touch of bile, squinted, rubbed his eyes hard with his thumbs, and dared open the bathroom door another half inch.

Smith had pulled a chair up to the table.

A napkin floated from the tray, snapped in the air, and settled on what would have been Smith's lap, if Smith had had one, which Stan didn't believe he did except for a pinkish right kneecap.

A mug of bitter levitated and tipped, and the dark liquid dribbled onto the floor.

"Well, damn!" a voice said with a laugh. "Boy, you'd forget your fool head if it wasn't screwed on."

The elastic bandages unwound themselves and flew toward a jacket propped under the window.

O horror, Stan thought in horror, and scuttled away from the door in disbelief and horror; horror, horror, horror, ohmygod horror.

He must have blacked out.

The next thing he knew, he was listening to Smith rage about the room, screaming about vile intruders, Hunnish invaders, the scum of the earth infiltrating his kingdom. Things crashed; things shattered; things broke and flew and crashed and shattered.

Stan, he thought as he crept back toward the door, pray the

mad bastard doesn't have to take a piss; and pray that you didn't see what you thought you didn't see.

The door flew open before he reached it.

Something grabbed him by the throat and yanked him cleanly off his feet.

"You!"

Stan managed a nod.

"Spy!"

Stan shook his head.

"Villain!"

Stan didn't know what to do. Legally he supposed he was; morally he was just a poor sod trying to make a living. And bunging it up swell too, if this was any indication.

Suddenly he was slammed against the wall, the breath knocked out of him; dazed, he slid to the floor and massaged his throbbing neck, refusing to believe it when the guitar drifted over toward the table and tilted itself.

A voice then, eerily calm, deep and almost familiar: "Do you know who I am, you low-down thief in the night?"

Stan nearly throttled himself to keep from babbling. "No, sir, I surely do not, no." He didn't know which way to look, so a good stare at the instrument was most likely better than staring at the kneecap.

A string was plucked; a note floated with the guitar.

"Do you recognize that?"

Stan closed his eyes tightly. He had gone mad, lost his mind, that's what it was.

"B-flat?"

A high-pitched laugh that tightened his roiling stomach, chilled his spine.

"Excellent! Excellent! For that, you little worm, you will die swiftly."

"The hell!" Stan sprang to his feet, from which position he was shoved back into the wall, his skull denting the plaster.

The voice again, cold and close: "And then I wrote:

Though whiskey drove my little darlin' to Glasgow,
'Twas a five-ton lorry done knocked her flat.

"Holy shit," said Stan. "That . . . you sound just like Racig Dargren, the Welsh Vagabond!"

A victorious peal of insane laughter.

Stan wanted to weep. "But you're dead!" he shouted.

The guitar dropped to the floor.

Someone hammered on the door.

"Do you know," said Racig Dargren evilly, "do you have any idea what your meddling has done?"

"Well, I wouldn't exactly call it meddling," Stan dared protest. "It was more in the line of—"

The voice rose slightly. "Do you know what turning up those burners, shaking those beakers, sniffing those test tubes has done to my work?"

Incredible, he thought; the guy would have to be invisible to know I'd done all that.

A test tube rose from the table, hovered, and flew against the wall, where it shattered like a gunshot, red-steaming liquid dripping ominously to the floor.

"Ruined!" the voice screamed.

Another one bounced off the door.

The hammering continued.

A beaker exploded when it was swept onto the threadbare carpet, and a noxious cloud of orange and yellow smoke billowed to the ceiling.

"Ruined! Ruined! Now I'll have to start all over!"

Stan cautiously eased himself to his feet and sidled toward the door. "Is it all that bad?" He pointed a quaking finger at the kneecap. "Seems like—"

"Bad? Bad?"

The insane cackling rose and fell, rose and fell.

The door shook on its hinges.

A rack of test tubes shattered against the hearth.

"Bad?"

The laughter.

The hammering.

Stan lunged for the doorknob, but he was grabbed and tossed aside. He struck out and hit nothing; a fist doubled him over. He punched at the kneecap; a foot caught him in the ribs. He fell, gasping and choking.

Then a voice in his ear: "My experiment may be dead for now, but not as dead as you're going to be, you white-bellied wife-stealer you!"

"Wife?"

Except for a few gurgles and screams, that was Stan's final word on the matter as invisible hands grasped him by the throat and pulled him off his feet. He kicked, he struggled, he grabbed those powerful invisible wrists and tried desperately to pry them loose, but to no avail.

He was carried to the door.

The door opened.

In the hall stood Flora Tatterall, hands on her hips, her face dark with anger.

"What the bloody—"

Then it was her turn to scream when she saw the floating, strangling man.

With hands up, she stumbled backward, and screamed again when the man, like a discarded puppet, was thrown down the stairs.

A voice screamed: "*Dead! Dead! You're all dead!*"

And the last thing the landlady heard before she fell into a faint was the maddened sound of bare feet thumping down the steps after the body.

◆ 4 ◆

"Angus?"

"Patience, love. We'll be there in a minute, or I'll know the reason why."

"Why?"

"Because then we'd be lost."

"We are?"

"Are what?"

"Lost."

"Of course not."

"But you just said—"

"Kiss me."

"No, that's not what you just said. You just said—"

"Kiss me, Lizzy. Quickly. Very quickly. And by the time we're done—"

Lord, Angus thought, when she threw herself into his lap, wrapped her arms around his neck, and clamped her lips to his; Lord.

Milo Yonker plopped himself down on a dry patch of grass and arranged his purple robe modestly about him.

His head ached.

His throat felt a little scratchy.

But his heart soared.

Through an incredible stroke of luck—taking a shortcut to Kirkie's flat through Rains Lane—he knew now what the woman in the red coat looked like, and as soon as Kirkie finished packing, they would stake themselves out at the Bowlingham. And wait.

The woman in the red coat would go there. He was sure of

104

it. As he had lain nearly dying on the street after that ingrate Dean had plonked him, as he lay in a daze during which a fair portion of his life had flashed before his closed eyes, he'd heard that foul name spoken. That very name which had been the bane of his entire life for the past few years. That same name which would deny him fame if he didn't take care of things once and for all.

Kent Montana.

And Kent Montana was staying at the Bowlingham.

And if Kent Montana was staying at the Bowlingham, it was a sure bet that the woman in the red coat and that ingrate Dean would go there to enlist the baron's help.

And when they did—

He giggled.

He shifted.

He waved delightedly as Gretchen ran into the trees, pursued by a dismounted motorcycle gang.

The hell with her, he thought; if she doesn't show up tonight, I can always use Kirkie.

Claudius Cana backed away from Rains Lane as soon as all the screaming and yelling and shouting and shrieking began. This was not the time to find out if Dargren had made an appearance there; this was the time to lay out a few investment pounds among the Merkleton underworld, in order to find out where that ingrate Dean was. For he was positive now that Dean had the woman who had the notebooks; and if he found one, he would surely find the other.

"Claudius, not so fast!"

"Time is short, pet. Only hours now until we launch our campaign."

"I'm hungry."

"And," he said, pointing to a poster on a telephone pole, "I still don't understand why the entertainment committee chose that fishmonger, Yonker, to sing at the sacrifice tonight."

Poetra waved her holder. "You don't have to, my hero. Golly, you're not going to be there anyway."

"I realize that. But I do have a reputation."

"Oh, let him sing!" she said airily. "By the time you're finished, he'll have to come to you for permission to tune his wretched guitar, or whatever that thing's called."

He stopped in the middle of the street.

He looked up at the sun beaming down on his pudgy face.

He looked at Poetra and said, "How'd you like to be an Empress, my angel?"

"Do I get to eat?"

"As much as you want."

"Then I accept."

He bowed.

"So can we eat now?"

The moment Kent stepped into the King's Hump, all hell broke loose, and he wondered why he wasn't surprised in the least.

People he had never seen before grabbed at his sleeves, tried to talk and yell and scream at him, all the while pushing and pulling and shoving and guiding him roughly forward along the bar. It was incredible. It was unnerving. He hadn't seen anything like it since the winter his mother had tried to burn the village down while he was playing Father Christmas for the island orphans, Heather and Hanna, and the melancholy echo of that fateful day heightened his senses, made rigid his muscles, and deepened his voice when he bellowed:

"Shut up!"

They did.

Except for Eddie the barman, who popped out from the side door and beckoned to him urgently.

"Hazel," Kent instructed as he strode toward Jones, "stay by the entrance, be sure no one leaves or comes in until I say different. Janice, come with me."

Hazel did as she was bidden.

Janice remained by his side as he pushed through the excited crowd.

At the door Eddie looked askance at the secret agent, but Kent merely said, "It's all right, she's with me," and stepped over the threshold.

In spite of the sunlight pouring into the pub, the lighting was dim here, the unpolished wood of the walls and crooked banister reflecting nothing of the horror he soon spotted crumpled in an untidy heap at the foot of the staircase. Upstairs, a woman screamed ceaselessly and, without being told, Janice leapt over the horror and ran to give what assistance she could.

Nervously Eddie wrung his hands on his half-apron. "We was arguing," he explained as Kent knelt beside the horror.

"Me and Flora, that is. That . . . that Mr. Smith, he was screaming and yelling and bashing things about and disturbing the
peace, so I tells her to call the coppers before he does damage.
She wouldn't do it. No, not her. She had to go up there herself
to talk to the man."

The screaming stopped at the crack of a well-placed slap.

"Next thing I know, there's all this screaming and yelling
and a bloody great crashing down the stairs." He grabbed
Kent's shoulder. "I thought it was her, y'know? Lord help me,
I thought it was her."

The screaming started again.

Kent poked at the horror until it resolved itself into the broken
body of Stan Yarkshore, known thief and sneak, but fairly
harmless when it came to violence and killing. And definitely
harmless now.

The screaming stopped at the crack of a slap.

"Where is this Mr. Smith, Eddie?" he asked as he rose to
his feet.

The barman looked fearfully upward.

"Ah . . ." Kent said.

Shit, he thought, but made his way to the landing after
ordering Eddie to let the hooker at the entrance know what had
happened.

A single light burned dimly in the hall.

Flora sat propped against the wall, legs akimbo, her cheeks
bright red, her fists crammed white-knuckled against her chat-
tering teeth. Janice, breathing heavily, glanced up at his approach and smiled that she had everything under control. He
nodded, looked at the battered door, and with a deep breath,
stepped inside.

"Well, I'll be damned," he whispered.

It was a laboratory. A fully equipped and relatively smashed
laboratory. With a guitar.

Picking his way through the smashed smoking beakers and
shattered steaming test tubes, he reached the window unscathed
except for some mild acid burns on his trousers, and noticed
immediately that the sash was down, and locked from the
inside. Beneath it, on a wood valet, was a gaudy jacket the
likes of which he had never seen before; closer examination
proved it had been jabbed dozens of times with what only could
have been a syringe.

He grunted his puzzlement.

He turned to face the room.

This was obviously the mysterious Invisible Man's lair, but the culprit himself was nowhere to be seen.

A shadow at the doorway caught his attention.

"Kent?"

"It's all right, Janice. He's gone."

"How can you tell?"

He tapped the side of his nose. "Would you stick around this place after smashing it all to hell, frightening a poor woman out of her wits, and murdering a helpless thief who had obviously broken in here to see what he could steal?"

"If I were invisible, why not?"

He stared at her, stared at the steaming, smoking, stinking, multicolor-lighted room, and said, "Right."

Within seconds he was at her side and pulling the door closed behind him. Flora was on her feet, her peasant blouse askew, Eddie standing defiantly beside her, one arm around her waist.

"Well?" he demanded.

Kent ignored him, instead walked over to the shaken landlady and asked gently, "Flora, what happened? What did you see?"

She screamed.

Eddie jumped back.

Kent reached for her arms.

Janice sprang between them and slapped her twice, once a cheek.

This time, however, Flora would not be mollified. She shoved through them with the strength of a hysteric and ran down the stairs, shrieking, "Murder! Murder!" all the way into the pub.

Before Kent could reach the stairs himself, there was the sound of a resounding slap.

Silence.

"Eddie, what did Miss Bloodlowe have to say?"

The barman frowned.

"The hooker, Eddie."

"Oh." He gathered himself. "Well, she likes my pecs. Work hard on them, of course, and she noticed that right away. Lots of them do." He smiled proudly.

Janice giggled. "It's the excitement," she said to Kent. "The man's feeling a bit peckish."

He glared.

Janice shrugged, turned to the confused barman and said,

"Don't mind him, Eddie. What else did she say?"

"Well, she complained about someone trying to pinch her bum, which I don't blame him because—"

"Damn!" Kent snapped, and hurried to the first floor. "He's gotten away, Janice! We've got to find him before he kills again!"

"But how?" she wanted to know, racing right behind him. "I know the sun is out, but he's—"

He spun around at the door and clamped a hand over her mouth. "Not a word," he cautioned quietly. "We don't want to start a panic."

When she nodded, he released her, looked sorrowfully at what remained of Stan Yarkshore, and stepped into the pub. It had crossed his mind that he didn't have the slightest idea what he was doing, or why, or what had to be done next; it had also crossed his mind that no one, in these circumstances, would know what they were doing since they were faced with a horror unique to the real world. So it wasn't all that bad. A bit on the nervous side, perhaps, and a bit more arrogant, maybe, that he should take charge like this when he didn't know what he was doing, or why, but somebody had to do it, or this sort of thing, gone unchecked, would decimate Merkleton's population before it knew what had happened.

Midway to the door, Zero Zuller took his arm.

"I seen him, your lordship," he said confidentially.

"Zero, for god's sake."

"But I did," insisted the blind man. "Parts of him anyway."

Janice touched the man's shoulder. "Parts of him?"

"That's right, miss," Zero said with an eager nod. "First I thought it was two squinty beady eyes starin' at me, makin' fun, so to speak, of my physical condition. Then I realized, in a flash, that they was kind of floatin', like." His fingers described vague images in the air in front of her chest. "Beggin' your pardon, miss, but I knew then they was his . . . well, they was . . . his . . . ."

"Nipples?" she suggested.

Zero blushed.

Kent snapped, "Jesus, Zero, you're blind, remember?"

"Course I remember," the blind man snapped back. "But I got eyes, ain't I?"

At that moment, Hazel called to them from the entrance. Kent, fearing for what was left of his sanity and hoping his agent wouldn't take too much longer, asked Janice to get the whole story from the blind man, then pushed through the milling crowd, calming them with his steady gaze, assuring them that all was under control and Flora, once she stopped screaming and came out of the Ladies, would be just fine.

Hazel pulled him outside.

"What?" Kent demanded.

"Listen," she ordered.

He did—to the traffic on the High Street, the muffled footsteps on the pavement, the Salvation Army band blasting away in the park, the long shriek of grating metal when an errant cab sideswiped a lamppost, Zero's eerie whistled rendition of "The High and the Mighty," the murmuring and muttering in the pub behind him.

"I don't hear anything."

"Exactly," she said.

A frown; a scratching at his neck.

"So?"

"The flower girl!"

"Oh," he whispered. "Oh . . . hell."

·5·

When Mary Shweet felt ambitious, which wasn't very often unless she was starving, she plied her floral trade outside the music clubs and trendy Druid nightspots around Mistletoe Mews and Oaktree Road. Intervals and the ends of the shows were the most profitable times, especially if the bands were a hit. People felt expansive. They looked forward to a late dinner. They felt guilty as hell when a ragged but not disgustingly dirty slip of a thing with a fringed shawl around her thin shoulders and a scarf covering her hair stood miserably at the curb and deferentially held out her handwoven basket of simple flowers for their inspection.

She seldom spoke save to say softly, "Thank you, good sir," and "God bless you, miss."

They loved the "God bless" part.

It made them feel so Christian.

But when all she needed was a few quid to keep the wolf from the door, she either trundled along to the train station and stood by the ticket window, sniffling sadly and humming sad tunes about children dying all over the world, or she reverted to her usual haunt—the shops and hotels along the High Street. The people there were almost always tourists who, while they might not feel guilty, certainly weren't sure about proper etiquette concerning a flower girl straight out of BBC Dickens. More often than not, they bought a random blossom while pretending to ask directions to a restaurant or particular pub.

Mary obliged.

Everyone was happy.

And her poor old mum and dad would be able to eat another

meal without having to sneak out and steal it from the garbage bins in the neighborhood.

Today, however, it looked like garbage cuisine again.

Unlike last night, when the fog had pretty much squelched any chance of her selling out the basket, she had hoped the rain would bring out the misery highlights in her pallid complexion and the coins from people's pockets.

But the sun had ruined everything.

Today being the last day of the Festival, most of the tourists had instantly flocked to the Green, getting in their last licks before tonight's celebration. And she didn't dare go there. Too bright it was; she didn't look quite so much like a waif when the sun was out; more like just another poor kid out to hustle a buck.

In fact, she'd only sold one flower since the rain had stopped and the fog had lifted, and if it hadn't been for her poor old mum and dad, sitting home all alone by the stingy fire and weaving genuine Druid sacrifice baskets, she would have left the Lane an hour ago.

In fact, if it hadn't been for her poor old mum and dad, she never would have come to this place again, starving or not.

Not after last night.

Not after that cruel person, whoever he was, had so terrified her that she'd run just about all the way home, nearly clipped by a cab and run over by a one-light lorry.

But her poor old mum and dad, and their poor old dying Scottie, needed medicine and food, and there was no getting around it—she had to return.

So, feeling not at all brave but knowing her childly duty, she stood in Rains Lane, midway between Wagner's Restaurant and the King's Hump, a huddled and tiny figure in the center of the uncaring cobblestones. Holding out her wares whenever someone approached, sighing a melancholic wheeze when they passed her by.

Maybe, she thought, they can't see me.

She coughed into a delicate fist.

She drew the shawl more snugly about her shoulders.

Maybe I blend in too well.

A decision: It might be a good thing to draw attention to herself, out here in the cold damp alley, if she were to sing again. They always enjoyed her singing; it made them feel so good when she smiled at them and gave them a verse of their favorite song or folk tune.

She smiled briefly; malnutrition hadn't dimmed her clever mind all that much yet.

And so what shall it be, then? she asked herself, and immediately chose "Greensleeves," her own personal favorite, and that of her poor old dad's.

She cleared her throat, thought for a moment, and then opened her mouth.

Her voice wasn't grand, not like her dad's before the consumption got him, but it was high and sweet and carried like a sparrow's song, a melancholy sound that blended with the shadows, echoed faintly off the brickwork walls, and filled those who passed her with a tenderness they'd not known since they were in their cradles.

> *Alas, my love, you do me wrong,*
> *To treat me so discourteously,*
> *When I have suffered oh so long,*
> *Delighting in your* AWK!

Fingers of ice wrapped tightly around her neck and mercilessly dragged her deeper into the alley, into the cloak of the shadows of the walls.

Her little heels drummed on the cobbles, her tattered basket flew from her hands and rolled onto its side, the fading blossoms spilling into dank puddles, and her shawl fluttered from her shoulders, the broken wing of a songbird whose voice has been forever stilled.

◆ 6 ◆

Kent was glad the fog had lifted. He didn't like the fog. Not only was it invisible in the dark, unlike a good streetlamp, but it reminded him of the heavy mists that crept ceaselessly across his ancestral island home and covered the occasional free-lance and always barmy assassin trying to get in good with his mother.

Plus, it tended to creep its clammy way down your neck and spine, settle on your hair and make it too heavy, and do things to footsteps and hushed voices that only happened in the dreams you wished you hadn't had when you woke up the next morning.

It also made hunting for dead bodies, or potentially dead bodies, much too difficult.

The shadows, however, weren't much better.

Though the sun shone with autumnal clarity on the High Street, the height of the buildings that formed the walls of Rains Lane prevented much light filtering down to the ground. Oh, it was bright enough to see by, but more like twilight than noon, even in the middle of summer. Which this wasn't, being late September.

Therefore, his eyes played tricks on him, making him see things that weren't there, and not see the thing he wanted to see that wasn't there. It made life hard.

Not to mention hunting for the murderer himself.

Which he promised himself he wouldn't, if nobody else did.

It took only a few minutes, most of it scouring walls and stoops and the occasional dustbin, to realize that unless they used several yards of fine-mesh netting, or nine fat women's net stockings, the killer in his nonvisible state could all too easily avoid them.

It was a waste of time.

What they clearly needed instead was some sort of plan, a viable and clever method of drawing the man out of hiding where, with some luck and a providential miracle, they'd be able to get him down and beat the shit out of him so he wouldn't be able to escape again.

Dispirited, verging on the disheartened and the hell with it, and fearing the worst for poor Mary Shweet, whose pathetic basket of flowers he had discovered abandoned beneath the cheerily lighted window of Wagner's, he pulled up his jacket collar, stuffed his hands in his pockets, and returned to the King's Hump, where Hazel already waited, her fur somewhat ratty, her padded shoulders slumped.

"Nothing," she reported.

He nodded; he expected nothing else. This entire matter was becoming too predictably depressing.

Janice came out of the pub then, spotted Hazel, and cupped a hand expertly around one ear. "I don't hear anything," she said with a worried frown.

"Yes," said Hazel.

"Oh dear."

"It looks like it."

Janice sniffed, and shrugged one shoulder. "And he was so nice too."

"Hey, I'm right here," Kent said over her shoulder, moved by her concern. "It was Mary the orphan flower girl that Hazel referred to."

The policewoman whirled, gasped in delight, and grinned. "You!"

He took her elbows, stared into her eyes, and winked. "Aye, it is."

The smile became a sappy grin. "I thought you were . . . I got the impression that . . ."

"So I gathered."

The grin broadened, and her tongue darted between her lips. "You want to lick my nose, your lordship?"

Hazel coughed.

Despite the implications and ramifications of nose-licking and tongue-darting, Kent understood resignedly that this was no time for a romantic interlude. Events had, for the time being, gone beyond the needs of mere man and woman. Which, when he thought further about it, was a hefty crock-and-a-half if he had ever heard one, but it was also too miserable out here for any sort of comfort.

He said instead, "What did Zero say?"

"He saw nipples."

"I heard that part. What else did he say?"

"They were brown."

"Nipples?" Hazel said.

"Don't ask," Kent suggested. He peered into the pub and shook his head slowly. "I was thinking just a bit ago that we cannot go on without a plan. Running around like this is going to get me dead and us nowhere. Fast."

"Sweaty, though," Janice said brightly, then winced. "Kent, you're hurting me!"

"Sorry." He released her and leaned a weary shoulder against the wall. "Look, I may be speaking out of turn, not being the professional and all, but perhaps we should go back to the man's room." He pointed upward. "You two are the experts here. You could conduct a thorough search, sift through the wreckage, with luck come up with some clues that might guide us. If we know who this bloke is, or why he's done this, maybe then we'll be able to come up with a way to trap him."

Reluctantly Hazel shook her curly head. "Searching is out, I'm afraid, your lordship."

"But why? That's . . . but it doesn't make any sense not to, does it?"

"Maybe, but we're hookers, see?" A look to Janice, who nodded slow confirmation. "We don't do the searching is what I mean. That's not us. We lure, we divert, we entrap, but we haven't had the searching parts yet." An apologetic shrug. "It's like doctors, you see."

"No," he said, resolved to be calm. "No, I'm afraid I don't see. At all."

"It's specialization, Kent," Janice explained. "We hook, others search."

"The nation must be proud," he answered sourly.

"Damn well ought to be," Hazel said bitterly. "It's been hell on my love life."

If I kill them, he thought, I will either be locked away for life for high treason, or I will be given a medal by the Queen herself, no questions asked and how's your mum, does she still collect Claymores? Then, through no fault of his own, he scowled at his uncharitable mood, shook it off unwillingly, and suggested to the now shivering agents that they repair to the Bowlingham lobby—it was quieter, they would be undisturbed, it was safer, and the three of them, working together, might be able to come up with something that they could use.

They agreed.

He was about to suggest further that they stop off at the grocery to get something to eat because he was absolutely starving to death, when suddenly the quiet was shattered by the roar of racing engines and several whooping sirens distinctly heading in this direction.

Swell, he thought; someone had finally had the presence of mind to call the police. Just what he needed—Herman Easewater and his confounded kneeling.

"Your lordship?"

The blind man stood unsteadily in the doorway, peering helplessly into the dim light, one palsied hand holding a bronze cashmere muffler close about his neck.

"What is it, Zero?"

"Not meanin' to disturb you, sir, but have you given any more thought to me new accordion?"

Two hookers and a blind nutter, he amended to his honors list; hell, they'll give me the effing country.

"No."

Zero touched his cap deferentially. "Just thought I'd ask, sir. My lips is getting tired is all."

Kent, smelling a con and wishing he'd take a bath, stuffed several bills into the blind man's eager hand. "Then wet them, Zero, and keep your eyes open." The sirens grew louder. "We'll be at the Bowlingham should you hear anything I might be interested in."

Zero Zuller folded the bills into his jacket pocket, saluted smartly, and strode back into the mob milling around the bar, demanding from Eddie this instant all the relevant details of the monster's attack on their favorite landlady, who still hadn't come out of the Ladies.

At the same time, Kent turned not so smartly on his heel and marched quickly toward the High Street, head down and face averted. He did not want the police to see him, much less question him. If he told them the truth, they'd lock him up; if he lied, they'd find out and lock him up.

Flashing blue lights.

A siren winding down.

He swung around the corner and smiled when Janice and Hazel, understanding his plight, each took firm hold of an elbow and leaned into him—just two friendly women holding up a friendly drunken friend.

But he stiffened when, just before the grocery where a bull-dog, unless it was Ethel, was savaging an orange, the way was blocked by a huge man in a wrinkled peacoat and slightly undone woolen cap.

It wasn't Easewater in disguise.

"You Kent Montana?" he growled.

"Easy, buster," Hazel warned.

Janice jutted her chin pugnaciously.

"I asked you a question!" the man demanded, ignoring the women.

Kent checked the surly stranger over, and finally, warily, nodded when he couldn't see any nipples.

"Good," the man said, and reached into his pocket. "I've got a little something for you."

· 7 ·

Colonel Lumet Braithe (Ret.) did not for a minute believe that he was as stupid as he looked. Far from it. It had taken him years to get where he was in the civilian world, and he knew damn well he hadn't done it all through luck. A little luck. That comes with the territory. But not a lot of luck. More than most, less than some, that was about the size of it.

But he was not going to depend on luck to tell what in heaven's name Kent Montana, of all people, was doing, sneaking around his hotel right out there in the open with a hooker who was dressed today as if she were a regular woman, and a hooker who at least had the decency to dress like a hooker, even if her fox fur was showing signs of wear and tear.

Things like this just weren't done in the Hotel Bowlingham.

Certainly not—he checked his watch—before four of a Saturday afternoon.

Definitely not on Festival weekend.

It made him look bad.

Not the hooker part, because he was canny enough to encourage them as long as they didn't get out of line and stopped conning their clients into buying them drinks in his lounge; the not knowing what it was all about, however, made his staff snicker and sneer and point at him behind his back. In the army they would have been flogged; in civilian life they got jobs and joined unions.

He leaned his considerable but not flabby by any means bulk against the groaning porter's desk and glared across the lobby into the lounge. They were there. His lordship, the two hookers, a woman in a truly offensive red coat, and a sailor who looked as if he'd never been at sea in his life. He would bet on that.

He knew his men when he saw them. Judging character was a good part of how he got where he was today, except for the luck, which wasn't all that great a player, though it certainly helped with his taxes.

Something was up.

Montana knew what it was.

The colonel didn't.

But he did know that something was up because of all the commotion in the ratty and ill-mannered King's Hump, the entrance of which he could see, as often as he could, from his top-floor-suite window. Masses of people lately running in and out, screaming and yelling, that damn fool blind man kicking the hell out of his squeeze box, and Inspector Bloody Easewater snooping around like a giant bloodhound.

It didn't take a two-by-four across the head to tell him something had happened.

And every time something happened, Montana and the hookers came back here after a while, drank in the lounge, and then something else happened.

He wanted to know what it was.

He had to know what it was.

There was the clean, crisp, heady, seductively illicit scent of money to be made about the whole suspicious business, he would swear to it, and he was determined to get at least one of his hands on some.

He reached into his waistcoat pocket and pulled out a silver tin of snuff. With practiced thumb and finger he snorted a pinch into each nostril, sneezed off his monocle, sniffed loudly, and wondered if a frontal assault would be best in this situation, or a clever flanking maneuver during which he would eavesdrop, collate information, and repair to his headquarters to devise his next move.

He sneezed again.

The cashier, working on the weekly figures at the registration counter, noticed his apparent distress and raced over with a box of tissues.

"Thank you, child," he said graciously.

She practically curtsied. "It's quite all right, Colonel. Anything to keep you healthy."

He watched as she walked away, sighed at the young, firm, unattainable female flesh encased in that fluffy white blouse and painfully snug black skirt, and immediately chided himself for being a disgusting and heartless sexist, an old-fashioned, lecherous pig who had nothing better to do than imagine his distaff employees, and a few of the local shop clerks, lolling about in his king-size bed with champagne glasses at their sides and roses in their teeth.

That would not do.

Well, it would; but it wouldn't.

She was, after all, help.

"Hands off" was his motto for the staff and some of the guests; dirty your hands on someone's else patch, Lumet you old fool, if you must dirty your hands at all.

Unfortunately he'd had a rather long run of bad luck in that particular department this month, give or take a season. And when the cashier stood once again at her post, glanced up from her figuring, and smiled prettily, it took all his strength and fiber to keep from pawing the carpet with his booted foot.

Steady, man. Steady.

A movement then at his peripheral vision made him focus again on the lounge. Montana was returning to his booth with a tray of drinks. The hookers were glum. He could not see the face of either the sailor or the other woman.

Montana looked absolutely grim.

It was then that the night porter, his uniform hidden by a topcoat the colonel had lent him, scuttled into the lobby, looked around in a panic, spotted the owner, and scuttled behind his desk.

"Well?" the colonel asked without taking his gaze from the group in the booth.

"Coppers all over the place, sir," the porter reported. "Seems there's a dead man."

"Dead man?"

"Yes, sir. Fell or was tossed down some stairs he was, broke every bone in his body."

"I see."

"Miss Tatterall is apparently hysterical."

The colonel nodded.

Montana sprang to his feet and waved his arms, sat, jumped up again, sat, and his expression suggested either a superior goosing or fatal news.

"Nipples."

Instinctively the colonel looked at the porter, cleared his throat noisily, and looked back at the bar. "Nipples, Reg?"

"That's what the blind man said."

"Nipples?"

"He saw them, he says. Says they was like beady brown eyes just hanging in the air, like."

"Nipples?"

The cashier ran over, concern muddying her fresh freckled complexion. "Sir, are you all right?"

"Nipples," the colonel muttered.

She blushed. "Sir?"

"Nipples," said Reg, the night porter. "That's what the blind man saw."

"Blind man?"

"Right. Nipples."

"Balls," said Petula Vanwort.

The colonel reared back, shocked, delighted, confused, red-faced; he only just managed to catch his monocle. "I beg your pardon?"

"That's what Etta and Ethel said."

"They did?"

The cashier nodded solemnly. "Last night it was, sir. Said they saw balls in their shop." Then she clasped her hands before her contritely. "If you'll pardon the language, sir."

"Well, my man saw nipples," said Reg.

"Your man was blind," the cashier countered.

"Balls," muttered the colonel.

"Hey," Reg protested, "I'm only telling you what he told me, sir."

With a one-handed chop at the air, the colonel silenced them both. He stroked his mustache, rubbed his chin, pulled at his nose, and tugged at an earlobe.

"Lads," he said, "something is afoot in the old Bowlingham, and that man"—he pointed at Kent—"is in the thick of it."

Petula paled. "But sir, that's—"

"Exactly," he told her. "A baron, two hookers, a sailor, and a woman with abominable taste in outerwear." He tapped the side of his nose knowingly. "Nevertheless, methinks there is a connection."

"Party," the night porter suggested. "It is the Festival, you know, sir."

"No. No, I don't think so." He slapped a palm on the desk. "Return to your positions. But be ready," he cautioned, "for

●

when I give the signal. Act quickly, and there'll be a fat bonus
in your paychecks this week.''

He strode briskly away across the lobby, adjusting jacket,
waistcoat, mustache, monocle; he stood at the lounge entrance
and allowed his paunch to bulge, his shoulders to slump, his
eyes to glaze over.

Then he stepped in.

The perfect two-sheets-to-the-wind retired colonel.

And with a little bit of good old British luck and military
savvy, by the time he was sober again, he would also be that
much richer.

''Kent,'' Janice scolded as she glanced around the room,
''will you please stop jumping up and down like that? You're
drawing notice to yourself.''

''Well, I can't help it,'' he protested, though he did manage
to keep his seat. ''I've never heard anything so insane in my
life.''

Angus Dean looked at him with pity and jabbed at the notebooks on the table. ''It's all right here, your lordship. You
cannot disbelieve the evidence of your eyes.''

He nearly laughed aloud. Here, in the very center of the
most civilized country in the entire known universe, and
France, in the very hotel that had become his home away from
home since his mother had mined the waters around his ancestral island and winery, with people all around him, Druids
on the loose in the streets, and the colonel staggering through
the door . . . here, in this place, they expected him to believe
the scribbled ravings of a lunatic.

It was ludicrous.

It was ridiculous.

It was impossible.

It was unthinkable.

If this were a movie, he'd walk out and demand a refund.

Then Hazel said, quietly, ''Remember poor old Stan and
poor little Mary.''

''We don't know that Mary's dead,'' he snapped.

A commotion at the door distracted him, and he groaned
when Ethel Queen rushed in, Archie the bulldog panting at her
heels. ''Murder!'' she screamed to no one in particular. ''Someone's murdered poor Mary Shweet!''

Instantly the bar emptied.

Hazel said, "Excuse me, I'm going to question the porter," and left.

Kent stared at the notebooks, looked across the glass-crowded table at Angus and Lizzy, and shrugged.

"Kent?" Janice said gently.

He looked.

"Remember the nipples."

He blinked.

He glanced up again and spotted three uniformed policemen racing up the street, one of them blowing his whistle all to hell, the other two brandishing their nightsticks. "All right, all right," he said reluctantly. "But in my room. We're too visible here."

Five minutes later, after a ride in the elevator he'd never forget, he was at his desk, Janice was in the chair at the foot of the bed, and Angus and Lizzy were on the bed itself, using the wall for a backrest.

"Nice place," Angus said. "Very cozy like."

Lizzy hushed him.

Janice kicked off her new shoes.

And Kent turned the notebook around, pulled it to him, and began to read aloud.

-V-

The Motivation

I wrote a new song last night, but the words will never be heard by any of my fans. BritWest Records have told me they no longer require the services of the voice that put them on the bleeding charts for eleven years in a row.

I am crushed.

I am ruined.

I shall drink tonight as I have never drunk before, and BWR will take full blame if anything happens to me.

I called my agent this morning, to find out the real reason why my contract has not been renewed. His secretary professes not to know my name. I had to go over there myself and threaten to throttle her before she let me in. My agent, whose name deserves no mention here, suggests that I either dye my hair or shave it off. Today's young Brit wants no part of the lives of ordinary men and women who love and cheat and laugh and cry and have babies and affairs and die of old age or a railroad crash. When he showed me out, I decided to find a new agent. By the end of the day, I learned a hard lesson—when you're out, you're out, and when you're out, you're out.

I believe I shall drink the sherry tonight, as all the whiskey seems to have been stolen.

My concert in Leeds has been canceled.

Two weeks sitting in record company offices. Two weeks of futility. No one is interested in the man who wrote ''(My Baby Was Lost) In Loch Ness Tonight.'' My Lord, has it all been for nothing?

• • •

This afternoon Tower Records have put me on a penny sale.

The final straw! My retirement funds have vanished! My investments have crashed through the basement floor! Did I really spend all my earnings on frivolity and false security? Was I really so vain to believe that I would last forever? I had to sell several of my handmade spangled costumes to a Covent Garden junk dealer in order to bolster the last few hundred pounds I withdrew from my account this afternoon. I fear that keeping it there will only leave it open to seizure.

I am drunk. I stagger about the flat like a drunk. I have no reason to live anymore.

A little girl asked me for an autograph today. I obliged, most gratefully, until she read it and began to cry. When I asked what the matter was, she said she thought I was Waylon Jennings.
Infamy, thy name is whatever it is.

My landlord has finally ousted me. I have sold everything I own in order to pay the rent. There is nothing left but my faithful guitar and an old suitcase bound with string. It is snowing out. Perhaps I shall freeze to death.

Singing about the joys of the open road is fine when you have a Jag; the real thing, I must say, is a pain in the ass.
The Lake District is most inhospitable this time of year. I manage to eat by playing tunes in whatever establishments will have me. Thankfully, many customers have heard of me. They wonder why I don't make a new record. When I tell them, they shrug and say, "That's show biz, guv."

I spent the night on the pebbled beach at Brighton. The tide nearly took me, a fisherman nearly took me, and three German tourists asked me where the best restaurant was. When I could not tell them, they stepped on my toes. I am bereft. All my calls to my former agent go unanswered. None of the other record companies will have me. Willie, Emmylou, Merle, and

Minnie have all interceded on my behalf, to no avail; they don't answer my calls anymore either.

I believe I shall kill myself.

I tried to end it all tonight, but I cannot swim and could not get far enough out to drown. I must think of something else before I lose my nerve.

> *Even though my true love is dirty,*
> *Wormwood Scrubs nobody clean.*

Needs work.

I passed through a small village today. I do not recollect its name. On a bench at the bus stop an elderly man sat with his wife. He sang her ''Lorry Lovin' Larry'' in a creaky old voice that made my heart break. I dared ask why he had done so. He told me it was their song. Though temptation whispered that I reveal my identity to them, reality suggested they wouldn't believe me. I am a proper mess indeed. I have not shaved in weeks, my clothes are clean but tattered, and my shoes are bound in newsprint in order to keep the cold and damp from my bunions.

I walked on.

There was no place for me here.

How cruel is the world wherein I live!

Late this afternoon, whilst I was standing by the edge of some moors, watching cattle graze and songbirds swoop out of the heavenly blue sky, I was set upon by some louts. They beat me to within an inch of my life, then left me on the verge to die. I did not die, more's the pity. When I returned to consciousness, it was dark and chilly. I struggled on and found this falling-down shack wherein I hope to die in comfort. I can barely see, I think my right arm is broken, I bleed from several cuts and gashes, and my hair has been pulled out in vicious clumps.

And they have stolen my guitar!!!

I am near death, and the instrument which makes my music is gone, therefore my music is dead.

What else can happen?

I dread to think.

• • •

Several days have passed since I last entered my innermost thoughts in these notebooks stolen from a newsagent. It has been a nightmare. Too weak to sit up, too weak to cry for help, I have been in a delirium. The clothes I have left are practically gone. They stole my shoes, and my toes look like claws. My hand trembles, I drool a lot, and I think I have gone deaf in my left ear.

I cough up blood and phlegm, and it hurts so much that I wish I were dead.

I tried to cut my wrists today, but the pencil point is too dull. Perhaps, with diligence, I can erase myself.

Angels came to take me away today. I was most willing to go, but they said I stank and ought to take a bath now and then, because the Lord, while He is truly merciful, is also of a most delicate nature.

I think I am going mad.

Angels have wings, but the wings aren't striped.

It came to me whilst I was supping on grubs and bark outside the shack.

> *My darlin' is the Queen of all I survey,*
> *The moors are her palace,*
> *Windsor Castle is where she goes when she wants to*
>   *have lunch with her brother and two sisters,*
> *And I am her Knight, unless I'm leavin' today on*
>   *the next train to Cardiff even though I don't*
>   *speak Welsh anymore.*

My inner voice tells me it's a little rough. I do not mind. As long as I can keep the words coming, as long as I can continue to speak from the heart, perhaps I will be able to retain what little grip I have left on my sanity.

I cannot stop coughing.

I think my left leg is going to fall off.

I am writing this on my bed of weeds and milkwort because I no longer have the strength to sit up, much less stand.

• • •

I am dying.

*Whoever reads this, should anyone find it and read it without
condemnation, I trust they will understand that it was BritWest
Records who have killed me in my prime. Not to mention those
so-called fans out there who stopped buying my records and
authorized biography as soon as I was canned.*

Nobody loves you when you're down and out of town.

Dying.

I cannot see.
All is dark.

Kent rubbed his eyes with his knuckles, pinched the bridge
of his nose, rubbed his eyes again, and wished aloud for a
good stiff drink. When no one moved to accommodate him,
so moved were they by what he had been reading, he wished
again, with a great show of coughing to prove his deprivation,
and Lizzy finally prodded Angus to his feet. Glumly the pseudo-
sailor took orders all around and skulked away.

No one said anything.

When the man returned with a tray of filled glasses, he said,
"No sign of the coppers yet. Looks t'me like them at the Hump
kept their mouths shut for a change. The colonel's blasted,
though."

Kent nodded and took a large whiskey for himself. After he
had gulped half of it down and wiped his eyes, he tapped the
notebook thoughtfully.

There was no doubt about it—the story he had read thus far
was, in his opinion, truly a pathetic one.

"This is pathetic," he grumbled.

From her chair, Janice clucked and scowled. "Kent! The
man is disintegrating before your very eyes—in his very own
words, mind you—and you call him pathetic?"

"Not that kind of pathetic," he said.

"I should hope not."

"Though," he added, "I might remind you that the man is
a murderer."

"Alleged," she corrected.

"He was seen!" he insisted.

"He's invisible!" she reminded.

"But—"

"Read on."

He looked to Angus and Lizzy for support, saw none forth-coming or even portending, and sighed. And when he dared ask Lizzy for a synopsis of what was to come, since she had obviously already been through the diary and knew its contents more thoroughly than he, she only begged him with a sorrowful expression to read for himself what had driven her, on pain of death, to seek him out in the city, in the fog. Another sip, a swallow, and he braced himself for the next portion. Based on what he already knew, he did not believe there would be many surprises. On the other hand, the guy was crackers, so you never know, do you?

The fever has passed.

I am not well by any means, but I am able, with the aid of a stout stick for a cane, to move about this wretched little shack in the middle of nowhere without falling down. I am tired of eating natural food. Tomorrow I shall wend my weary way toward the nearest town to see what alms I may beg from those who still remember who I am. A miserable ex-istence, a far cry from what I have been used to, but perhaps I can pull together the tattered remains of my life and launch a new career.

Shame! Woe! Misery!

The last of my dreams has been crushed!

After four solid days plodding through the driving rain and mud, I walked into a nondescript village, established myself at the only pub, and . . . they would not serve me! They would not! No one spoke to me, no one listened to my feeble attempts at a cappella singing, and one dolt dared claim that I was not who I claimed I was because Racig Dargren would never let himself fall to such a state!

If only he knew.

If only I had known.

The way these people treated me today, I might as well be bloody invisible.

My guitar is back!

I was, shame of shames, rummaging through a dustbin at the edge of a smallish town when, miracle of miracles, there was my guitar! Old Faithful, Old Blue, True Blue, my only

*true companion all these years! Those ruffians who had ac-
costed me obviously knew not its value and simply tossed it
away.*

*As I have been tossed by the arbiters of public taste and the
molders of contemporary culture.*

I live!
I sing!
I shall persevere!

I will kill myself today.
*After much struggling to tune the guitar, I opened my mouth
for a verse or two of "The Biscuit Is Hard but the Coal Miner's
Harder" and—nothing! Nothing! My voice has been ruined by
those weeks of illness, and I can do no better than a hoarse
croaking. No one listens. No one cares.*

I shall say it again—I may as well be invisible.

I WILL be invisible!
I have a plan!
*It came to me in the night, shortly after I had eaten the rat
poison I scrounged from the back of a careless chemist's shop.*

*Why, I asked myself, should I simply creep away into the
wilderness and leave behind those who ruined me fat and rich
and caring not for what they have done? Why, I asked further,
should I not extract my own pound of flesh? How, I concluded,
shall I do this thing?*

It is simple.

*As soon as I stop vomiting the rat poison out of my system
(a trick I learned in my carefree undergraduate days), I shall
return without qualms to that which supported me before I
became an internationally known country-and-western balladeer—chemical, biological, and physiological research!*

Why didn't I think of it before?

*It must have been the poison; poison will do that to a person
if they're not careful.*

I shall begin tomorrow.
And I WILL succeed!
Hahahahahahahahahahahahahahahahahahahahahahahaha.

*I have taken over a deserted farmhouse in Y——. I have
cleaned up the parlor, flushed out the pump, and have already*

made forays into several nearby towns in order to procure the equipment I need.

Tomorrow I begin.

It's incredible what one cannot remember from one's younger days, and, by the same token, how much one does remember, but falsely. When I finally put the fire out, I realized that I ought to study just a little more, just to bring myself up to date—tone up the old cranial muscles, so to speak. So I stole a few library books. Fascinating what they've come up with these past thirty years. But it is all grist for the vengeful mill, and I will not be stopped. The road is long, the way is hard, the table's on fire again.

[Later]

It's a damn good thing, during all the excitement, that I remembered that I am a genius. Otherwise I would probably be quite discouraged at this point. I shall sleep well, however, knowing that on the morrow I will either get the first batch right or blow myself up in the attempt. Nay, Racig, nay— you're being too pessimistic. Goodnight, sweet world! Your ass is mine in the morning.

> *Darlin', how can you see me*
> *When you can't even see me,*
> *Pinin' here alone for love*
> *Of your touch and a cup of that soup*
> *You used to make when we were young*
> *And so in love and you could see me*
> *Everyday blues.*

Despite the setbacks and the loss of my trademark eyebrows, I am heartened by the guitar and the new song. Surely I haven't lost it. And even if I have, I know it's around here somewhere.

So many weeks, so many failures.
Am I mad to think I can do this thing?

So close! So close!
And yet so far away.

I grow weary, but something burning inside me keeps me going. Today, for example, I nearly made the table vanish, but the acid beat me to it. One bloody burp. What the hell, I'll work on the floor.

The pigeon is invisible!
Sonofabitch, I did it!
There are some drawbacks, however. Since I couldn't see it, I stepped on it. A horrid sound, but a true martyr to the cause. Someday there will be a statue erected to that bird, I swear it.

Damn! The local constabulary have been making inquiries in the neighborhood. I fear my raids on the local pharmaceutical firms and such have drawn unwelcome attention. I shall have to be careful.
The bull is invisible. No problem not stepping on that one.

The police are too close.
Something must be done.
I dare not be too hasty, but neither can I allow them to interrupt the most important stages of my experimentation. I must find a way to elude them.

The bull died.
A lorry smacked into it. The driver was most astonished.

Dear God, the police were here today. Not inside, but nosing around the grounds.
I fear for my life.

There is an unforseen problem, and I do not know if I shall have the time to correct it.
While testing the last batch of formula (an attempt to speed up what I have already perfected), I have discovered that the tail on the rat I caught for lunch refused to vanish! And Mr. Supper Rat would not render his snout invisible with the rest of him!
I dread to think what Mr. Breakfast Mole will leave behind.
But I shall persevere.
And if not, I'll figure out a way to make cotton disappear. I'd better, or it'll be damn cold out there.

They surround the farmhouse.
A helicopter whirls overhead.
Someone with a loud-hailer demands that I surrender myself.
Spotlights stream through my windows.
Did that damn pigeon belong to someone?
There is only one thing I can do.

This shall be my last entry. Then I will give these notebooks to that cute little slut down at the library. I think she likes me. I know I like her. And I know she will do what is right with these precious notes.
A warning!

Heed yourselves, you citizens of the world! Look behind you! Look above you! Look under you! For I am coming to exact my pound of flesh! And when I am done, ye shall be undone, and rare shall be the person who doth not fall under my wrath!

Beware Red Festival Night!

Beware!

I am coming, world! And you ain't never heard me sing until you've heard my death song!

Peek-a-boo, suckers.

-VI-

The Reaction to the
Motivation

⋄ 1 ⋄

"Preposterous!"

Kent nodded his satisfaction. That was truly a good word; not the sort of violet-and-pansy double-entendre crap butlers were forced against their wills by impudent directors to say in daytime dramas. He liked it; he really liked it. As he thumped his chair around to face the others, he listened to the fading sound of it, the ring of it in the small room, and decided that it was . . . right. Aristocratic without being condescending, emphatic without being bullheaded.

It suited him; it more than suited the situation.

"Preposterous!"

Janice's foot met his shin on a cautionary basis. "Don't be silly, Kent," she said. "You saw what you didn't see, right? How can you deny that?"

Angus simply glowered; Lizzy rubbed her hands apprehensively.

"I didn't meant the invisible part," Kent said. "That much is beyond doubt."

"Then what's the problem? We haven't got a lot of time, you know."

"What does time have to do with it.?"

"Well," she said, "it seems you have forgotten that Racig Dargren made his singing debut *right here in Merkleton!*"

"Hey," he retorted, "I knew that. I was here, in fact."

"Oh, you were? Then do you also remember that his debut came *during the celebration on the last night of the Red Moon Festival*?"

Using his posture to retort that he damn well did remember, he also realized that Dargren was bent on some sort of homicidal

138

retribution other than the one proclaimed against him; and in realizing that, and after checking his watch, he also damn well knew that time was of the essence if they were to save the village from horrid destruction.

And himself, in the bargain.

"So what's the problem?" Janice said, nearly shouting.

"Well, if you must know," he answered rather stiffly, "first, I find it rather difficult to swallow that a deranged man who sings stuff like this can discover a formula which can render him reasonably unseen to human eyes. Especially when he can't even make his clothes invisible too."

"He bashed you with a pipe," she reminded him.

"Well, there is that, I suppose." He tapped the notebook against his knee and considered the odds of his own abrupt descent into temporary insanity. Not liking the figures, he cleared his throat instead. "All right. All right. It's against my better nature, mind, but I'll give the man that."

Angus grunted his approval.

Janice applauded him mockingly.

And Lizzy said, "But what about the other thing?"

"What other thing?" Kent said.

"The other preposterous thing."

He tossed the notebook into Janice's lap. "I don't know if it's significant or not," was his admission. "It may not be. But I fail to see how a man, in fear of his life, in the throes of blossoming madness, can write—with a stubby pencil, mind you—in goddamn bloody *italics*."

There was a silence.

A siren outside.

"It's not significant," Janice finally decided.

"Okay," he said. "Just so I know."

He stood, glanced around and realized there was no room to pace, and sat again. One foot tapped. His left hand covered one cheek. His eyes narrowed in concentration. It was apparent that Dargren had finally lost whatever control he might have had, that wholesale terror would continue to be the business of the weekend unless he and these three did something about it. But in order to do something about it, they had to know what the man was going to do next, aside from killing someone else. And since they had no idea what in hell he was going to do next, and since it was clear that they themselves had been marked for death by their participation in this affair, and since it was more than evident that they would probably have to hide out in this room for God knew how long, he wondered if he'd have to sleep on the floor again, or if he could toss Angus for the bathtub.

"We'll have to set a trap," Janice said.

Damn, he thought.

"It's the only way," she explained to the others.

"I agree," said Angus firmly, drawing Lizzy into the protection of his arm. "The time for lurking is behind us."

Damn, he thought again.

"So what I suggest is this," she continued. "We let Kent here go out—"

"Whoa now!" he protested. "Don't I have a say in this? I might have a few ideas, you know."

"Maybe you do," she conceded, "but you're the hero, so you're going to end up doing it anyway, so why waste our valuable time interrupting when we could be getting on with it?"

Damn, he thought a third time.

Janice rose, smoothed the wrinkles from her skirt, walked to the bathroom door, and leaned against it, her arms folded in an official manner across her breasts.

The door clicked open.

She fell onto the tiles.

"It's all right," she said when Kent made to rise. "I'm thinking, that's all."

He glanced over his shoulder into the mirror, where his reflection suggested that a swift and permanent suicide might be in order if he wanted to get out of this alive.

"We will break up into teams," Janice announced from the floor, pointing at the ceiling as if she were using a diagram. "Angus and Lizzy, myself and Hazel. Once we are in position, Kent, on my signal, will begin walking toward . . . oh . . . the Ringstones place. What the hell. Lots of people down there, you see, the tourists and such. We will follow unobtrusively. Behind the trees, stuff like that." The finger pointed at the sink. "We will each carry a can of shaving cream. When Racig makes his move, we will move in, spray him, expose him, grab him, and arrest him." The finger moved to jab at Kent. "His lordship will be safe, we will have the Invisible Man in custody, and Merkleton will be spared."

Angus slapped his legs in approval. "Excellent! No lurking

about. That's good. Right to the heart of the matter. Very good. Very good indeed.''

Janice crossed her legs at the ankles. "Thank you."

Kent said, "Excuse me."

Lizzy said, "Will I get to carry the can?"

"Of course," Angus assured her. "You carry the can, I shall provide the muscle."

Kent cleared his throat. "I say."

"Thank you, darling."

"Good thinking," said Janice from the bathroom floor.

"I have a question," Kent said. Loudly.

They looked at him, frowning.

"Among other things," he began in his best reasonable manner just this side of screaming, "how do we know he'll follow me? He has all of Merkleton to destroy, remember?"

"Oh, that's easy," Janice replied. "You'll pretend to be a little drunk, weave around a little, and sing some of his songs. He won't be able to resist. By defaming that which he holds most dear, you will become the symbol of all he hates and despises; you will be the symbolic Merkleton of his demise and burial; you will embody all that he wishes to avenge."

"And how," he said tightly, "do you reckon all that?"

"Ask Lizzy."

He did.

Lizzy shrank apologetically against the wall, and his eyes widened in sudden comprehension. "I'll be damned," he said. "You know all about him, don't you? You know how he thinks, isn't that right? You know it because *you're the notebook slut!*"

After Angus hit him, he tumbled from the chair onto his back and discovered what had made the ceiling so fascinating for Janice—all those nebulae and comets, all those pretty lights, tracing patterns of the future to guide him on his way.

Incredible.

"On your feet," Angus growled, fists at the pugilistic ready. "Lordship or no lordship, I'm gonna kick your bleedin' ass all the way to Bath."

"No!" Lizzy said tearfully. Then, more quietly: "No, Angus. Don't hit him. He's right."

"He is?" Angus turned, shocked. "Do you mean you're the slut?"

"Hit him," Kent whispered dizzily. "Somebody hit him."

The woman lowered her head, folded her hands in her lap.

"Yes. Yes, it's true—I was the librarian in Y——." She paused for a collective gasp. "He used to come in of an afternoon, Mr. Dargren did, chat me up a little when I was alone, pump me for vital information about biophysics and things. Mrs. Q——, my superior, didn't much care for him, but I suppose he took a fancy to me." Her fingers tented beneath her chin. "I didn't know who he was, not at first. But he was always singing the same songs to himself while he studied or stole my books. It wasn't long before I put two and two together." She looked up, her eyes moist, her lower lip aquiver. "It was too late by then, of course, to do anything about it. He came running in one day and thrust the notebooks at me, told me he'd see me soon though I would never see him again, and ran out. The next thing I knew, there'd been a terrible battle at the old farmhouse. Then I read . . . I read his notes and knew there was only one person in the world who could stop him."

Kent, who was staring at the ceiling, said, "Are you looking at me?"

"Yes, your lordship."

The curse, he thought, of an agent who doesn't send me scripts with a touch of Shakespeare, a dollop of Marlowe, a soupçon of Soupy Sales.

As the stars faded, he turned his head to one side and stared at the soles of Janice's feet.

"Are you looking up my skirt?" she demanded.

Sighing, he returned his gaze to the ceiling, listened as Lizzy sobbed and Angus comforted her; listened at the street filled with the wail of an ambulance; listened to the blood that raced through his veins, to the ghastly warnings of his self-preservation mode, to the subliminal voice of the city he loved pleading for salvation.

Not to mention his own life, which, until now, had been pretty much in his own control except for the times when his mother got pissed.

He sat up.

Janice sat up.

Angus released Lizzy.

Lizzy pulled down her skirt.

Then he stood, stared at each one in turn, and said in his best authoritative voice, "I have a gun in my suitcase. It is loaded, highly illegal, and terribly convenient. If one of you, just one of you, ruins my coat with that goddamn shaving cream, I'll blow your effing head off."

There was a knock on the door.

No one moved.

If I had any brains, he thought, I would climb out the window and learn to fly to Brazil.

Lizzy, ever helpful as was her librarian nature, wriggled off the bed and took hold of the knob. "Who's there?" she asked politely.

"Room service," came the muffled reply.

As she began to turn the knob, Kent ordered "No!" in a harsh whisper. "It's a trap, Lizzy." With a look to the others to keep silent, he plunged his hands into the wardrobe, fumbled through his jackets and trousers, and finally pulled back with a gun in his hand. "Stand back. I'll get him through the door."

"Och, don't be daft," chided Angus with a chuckle as he huffed himself to his feet. "I ordered another round before I came back." He smiled tolerantly. "You're a nervous one, aren't you?"

"I've been beaned," Kent reminded him. "With a steel pipe."

"Ah. But not to worry, your lordship. Well in hand, well in hand."

Gently he eased Lizzy aside and opened the door.

Kent raised his arm and cocked the hammer.

"Ah," Angus said again.

There was the tray, properly laden with drink, just as he had ordered.

There was also a pair of bloodshot eyeballs, and not a hell of a lot else.

With a startled gasp, the would-be sailor grabbed the door and tried to slam it shut, but Racig Dargren was swifter—he threw the tray into the man's unsuspecting face and kicked the door out of his hands.

Kent fired twice.

Lizzy screamed.

And the small room echoed with the high-pitched laugh of a man who has seen madness . . . and the helpless target of his revenge.

Hazel Bloodlowe sat on the night porter's desk, her legs daintily crossed, her requisitioned fox fur open to expose a

low-cut, snug, rather translucent blouse and a belt wide enough
to strangle a jackass. She fluffed her hair, checked her makeup
in her compact mirror, and glanced over at the cloakroom door.
Which was still closed, and had been for quite some time now.
She hoped that Reg Olifer wouldn't be too much longer. He
was an intriguing little man, but lacking in stamina and recu-
perative powers. A shame, really. He was the first man in half
a decade who had been able to—

A gunshot.

Another close behind.

Instantly she sprang from the desk and ran to the elevator
bank. The left one was in use, its polished chromium door
sealed against accidental opening and a backbreaking lawsuit.
The right one, however, stood open to the lobby, and it was
from that narrow shaft that she had heard the shots.

A third shot, so distant an untrained ear might not have
known what it was.

Quickly she checked the digital counter above the other elevator and noted with increasing horror that it indicated the top
floor.

Kent Montana's floor.

Without hesitation, her well-trained constabular reflexes
flung her into the open car, where she pressed the last button
before realizing she probably ought to have left a note for Reg,
just in case he recovered. As the door cranked closed and the
elevator began its ascent, however, she shrugged the nicety off
and rummaged frantically through her voluminous purse,
searching for either the illegal handgun she always carried when
she had to dress like a hooker or the personalized, mother-of-
pearl switchblade she generally carried as personal protection
when she wasn't on duty.

The knife came out first.

She planted herself in front of the door and flicked out the
gleaming, eight-inch, oft-sharpened blade.

The car rose.

She loosened her shoulders, flexed her legs, blew out a breath
to calm herself.

She could not understand how anyone had gotten past her.
Through a devilishly clever arrangement of tiny mirrors Reg
had installed in the cloakroom, she had been able to keep an
eye on the lobby the entire time he was ruffling her fur and,

as her mum had often amusingly put it, passing the baton. No one had come in; no one had gone out.

The car rose.

Hang on, Janice, she pleaded silently as she watched the numbers change maddeningly slowly; hang on, girl, don't let the bastard get you.

The car slowed.

She loosened her shoulders, flexed her legs, moistened her lips in case it was a false alarm, and stared at her reflection in the metal door.

She fluffed her hair quickly.

The car juddered to a halt.

She took a deep breath, and as soon as the door cranked open, she leapt into the hall.

Petula Vanwort fluttered and dithered behind the registration counter. Dilemmas didn't suit her, not at all, and she wished the colonel hadn't placed such a high trust in her abilities to sift through the mundane to the pith of the moment. It was, to be sure, an honor, but right now she wished he had bestowed it upon someone else.

What bothered her, what had flustered her into such a high state of anxiety that her cheeks flushed and her knuckles popped, wasn't Reg's vanishing into the cloakroom. He often did that of a slow day, with no slack in service or detriment to the hotel at large.

And it wasn't the hooker who had been sitting brazenly on Reg's desk, fussing with her hair, her fur coat, her makeup, and whatever else hookers fussed with while they were taking a breather. Petula understood full well that a well-placed hooker now and then managed to bring a sprightly contrast to the sometimes stodgy demeanor of the Bowlingham, and it was not her place to condemn the colonel's well-thought encouragement of that occasional lapse into titillating management.

No; it was the way the hooker had suddenly cocked her head, jumped from the desk, and fairly sprang into the elevator.

That bothered her.

That unnerved her.

For surely, she thought, this might possibly be the very thing which the colonel had cautioned her and Reg about before he had lumbered off into the bar. If it was, she had no business standing here doing the receipts and skimming a few quid off

the top for her old age; on the other hand, if it wasn't, if she
made a fool of herself by reporting what she had seen, she
could very well be back on the cruel streets without so much
as a by-your-leave, soliciting pennies from perfectly awful
strangers in order to keep herself in clothes and food and a
decent roof over her head until she found yet another position
suitable to her talents and temperament.

She dithered.

She fluttered.

She considered running into the bar to tell the colonel what
she had seen, just in case what she had seen was something
the colonel would want to know that she had seen. It would
be a coup if she was right; it would be a disaster if she was
wrong. And she shuddered at the thought of him dressing her
down in front of the entire staff, making her ashamed, forcing
her to forget the incredible, if somewhat disgusting things he
could do with that military paunch when he was in the mood
and she had downed her nightly glass of sherry at a gulp.

Petula, she commanded then, get moving! The colonel is
counting on you.

One final dither, and she raced around the counter into a
small alcove between it and the bar, plunged into the oversize
interior of the service elevator, raced out again and across the
lobby to the other elevators to check on the floor indicated by
the digital numbers, sprinted back across the lobby and into
the service elevator, where she punched the button that indicated the top floor.

The door closed smoothly and swiftly.

The oversize car rose without so much as a hiccup.

Praying that she wasn't being precipitous or foolish, she
tapped her foot nervously and just barely refrained from chewing her nails.

A moment later, just as she glided past the seventh floor,
she heard what sounded like a backfiring automobile, which
she knew instinctively couldn't be, because the service elevator, while large, wasn't large enough to hold a vehicle, even
if it had gotten into the hotel without her noticing, which it
hadn't, so it couldn't have been a backfire.

The oversize car rose.

She wondered how the colonel would reward her if she were
correct in her handling of the situation, and hoped with a quick
giggle that he would do the thing with the monocle, which was

even more amazing than the thing with his paunch.

The oversize car slowed.

She steadied herself, straightened her back, touched at her hair to make sure nothing was out of place.

The elevator stopped.

The door slid open without a sound.

A deep breath, and Petula Vanwort stepped boldly into the hall.

-VII-

The Terror Continues

◆ 1 ◆

Pandemonium, Kent Montana decided, was another pretty good word that imported butlers in continuing daytime dramas hardly ever got to use; and with, under the present circumstances and considering the non-explosive nature of garden parties, bloody good reason.

His third shot had loosened considerable amounts of ceiling plaster when Angus had tumbled into him on his flailing way to the floor, and the retired soldier in sailor's clothing lay there now, clawing at his liquor-burned eyes and moaning curses of a Near Eastern nature.

Lizzy, in her innocence, had been knocked heels over head onto the bed by the door, where in the course of her travels her skull had struck the wall in mid-somersault and crossed her violet eyes.

And Janice had leapt onto the chair, where, from the mysterious recesses of her bosom, she had extracted a revolver, which she aimed at everything she could aim at.

"I can't see him!" she cried.

Neither could Kent, and there was an excruciating frisson of panic tinged with impending mortality until the spunky constable courageously sprang into the bathroom and, a moment later, reappeared to declare it orb free. A swift check of the wardrobe without mussing his clothes produced similar results, and he quickly climbed over Dean's prostrate form to peer down the hall to his right.

"There!" he yelled, and sprinted out of the room into the narrow hallway. "Follow those eyeballs!"

He could hear Janice right behind him, could see those hellish spheres bobbing and weaving, rising and falling, then shouted at Hazel to hold the elevator when she leapt out of the car and nearly punctured his performance with the smallest sword he had ever seen.

The eyeballs raced on.

Doors opened, guests peered out, gasped, gaped, and locked themselves in.

Kent followed without bothering to offer explanations, slowly gaining ground on the Welsh Vagabond and trying to imagine some sort of male form below the obscenely exposed occipital organs so that, when he was close enough, he'd be able to tackle it if he didn't shoot himself first.

Dargren dared a glance behind him, and Kent raised his gun. "Halt!"

The eyeballs raced on.

A mad cackling spread in their wake.

A few yards ahead, the hallway ended with an abrupt jog to the left, and Dargren's eyes rounded it sharply, a faint thump and Welsh curse indicating that he had struck the wall with his shoulder.

Kent was only a few paces behind, but when he too swerved into the hall's next leg, he stopped, instantly recognizing a dire situation.

A young woman dressed in the Bowlingham black and white staff uniform sort of dangled outside the gaping door of the service elevator, her back arched, hands clutching at her throat, her mouth open in a silent scream. Above her head, the demonic eyeballs glared at him.

Kent aimed his weapon. "Leave her alone, Dargren," he warned. "She's not part of this."

A cackle; a snort.

The woman whimpered.

"You can't hit me without hitting her, Montana," Dargren taunted with exasperating truth. "One step closer and I'll cut her lovely throat."

Janice careened around the corner and dropped immediately to a stiff-armed shooting stance.

"You haven't got a knife," Kent said.

"I do so!"

"No, you don't. If you had, I'd be able to see it."

The eyeballs narrowed. "Okay, then I'll choke her."

Petula Vanwort gurgled as the invisible grip tightened around her neck.

"You can't get away, Dargren," Janice informed him coldly. "Police Constable Plase here. Give yourself up. It'll be for the best. I swear I'll put in a good word for you, cooperation and all that."

The cackle again, chilling and ominous.

"You have a gun," Kent noted as his mind searched for the key to unlocking this diabolical tableau.

"I do," she answered without taking her gaze off her target.

"I thought you police weren't—"

"Special circumstance," she responded bluntly. "Now, look here, Dargren, I don't want to have to shoot you."

Another laugh, this one so evil Kent felt himself shiver.

In the background the hushed voices of guests speculating behind locked doors on the scene in the hall and how it would affect their attendance at the party.

The helpless cashier kicked her feet feebly as she was dragged closer to the elevator entrance. It was clear she was on the verge of unconsciousness, and though Kent was no expert, he didn't think her color was all that good either.

Janice inched forward.

Stall him, Kent decided; let the cop get a clear shot at whatever the hell she was pointing that thing at; his own gun was useless.

"Dargren!" he snapped.

One of the eyeballs winked at him and didn't return.

Kent spread his arms. "Why me? I don't get it. I've read your notes, you know. You're a brilliant man, a consummate artist, a man with a purpose who should be channeling his energies into the betterment of mankind. I can understand your disappointment with BritWest Records, but why Merkleton? Why me? Was it luck? Chance? Coincidence? My head still hurts, Dargren, and I want to know why."

"I hit you with a pipe," the Invisible Man chortled.

Kent smiled gamely. "And a sense of humor too."

"Besides," the singer continued, "I overheard your conversation in there. I know you know why I'm back here. I know you know that my first triumph will . . . heh heh heh . . . soon be repeated."

"All right," Kent said, trying to keep Janice in sight so he'd know when to duck when she started blasting away, which he prayed wouldn't be all that long from now. "But that doesn't explain your concern with me. I mean, man, why the hell are you picking on me? I haven't done anything to you. I don't even know you."

"Actually you do, m'lord," Janice said from her firing position.

"Well, I know that I do," he snapped. "I meant that I don't know him personally."

"All the more reason for me to kill you!" the Welsh Vagabond screamed, so loudly that the cashier was nearly brought back to full consciousness.

"But that doesn't make sense," Kent retorted angrily.

Dargren laughed. "Oh, doesn't it, now? Well, let me tell you something, Mr. Baron Butler Two-bit Actor—"

"Hey," Kent warned.

"—*you* are the one who ended all that I have dreamt of, worked for, struggled for. This Druid-infested town is where I sang my first compositions, at the Red Moon Festival, and *you* are the one who stilled those songs in my heart!

"Forever!"

Kent blinked.

A bruised, scabby elbow appeared beneath the night clerk's chin.

"Me?"

The chortle grew into an insane high-pitched giggling. "Don't deny it, toff!"

Kent felt his gun waver. "Me?"

"You, you scum! *You* own the company. *You* told them to can me. *You,* you bastard! I saw the memos! I saw the letters! It was you! You! *You are the cause!*"

Kent blinked again. "Me?"

Petula sagged again, a dead weight which he prayed was only an unfortunate figure of speech.

Janice, who had moved a yard or two beyond him, looked over her shoulder. "You?"

"Him!" Dargren bellowed.

The denial was at his lips, formed and ready to be vocalized with all the indignation he could muster, when, with a metaphorical snap of his fingers, he recognized the diabolical hand of his mother, even if it didn't show up on the Invisible Man.

Oh hell, he thought.

Not, of course, that she could have been aware of Racig Dargren's mad obsession with invisibility, though she probably would have funded it had she known; but she must have secretly purchased a controlling share of the vast entertainment company in his name, then passed down the word that certain popular, if somewhat aging artists of a country and western nature were to be summarily released from their contracts. Bugger off, cowpoke, and don't forget your guitar. The fallout from such a shocking and seemingly callous decision would ruin Kent's hard-fought reputation—not in the business world, for he had no reputation to speak of there, but in the very business of entertainment wherein he had laid the foundations of the profession his mother so hated.

Supreme ostracism would be the result, with no venue for appeal.

No one would ever hire him again.

No one would ever see his face on the screen again.

He would be blacklisted, shunned, and forced into financial, personal, and emotional ruin; *Passions and Power* would forever remain the pinnacle of his success.

Of course, it could all be a crock as well; but for the time being, it served to explain why he was, as he had first thought, one of the primary targets of this loon whose second eye winked out even as he watched.

"Could be," Janice said thoughtfully.

"Could be?" Dargren yelled. "Could be?" Petula fairly quaked with his indignation. "The bloody effing sonofabitch *is* responsible, I tell you, and the unrecorded sales of millions are now on his hands!"

That laughter again, rising and falling, echoing off the walls, cascading throughout the building.

Until Petula Vanwort was flung across the hallway, and the elbow vanished into the elevator.

Kent raced for the door.

Janice crawled for the cashier.

The door closed.

And the last thing Kent heard was the mocking refrain "Oh, catch me if you can, Baron my lad, but when I catch you, you'll know you've been bad."

Jesus, he thought with a grimace.

Then he whirled.

"To the other elevator!" he cried. "We'll trap him in the lobby!"

· 2 ·

By the time Liz had cleared Angus' eyes with palmfuls of cold water, and he had managed to convince her that no, they would not have to buy a German shepherd and a special parking license, the hall was filled with a racket the likes of which she hadn't heard since the afternoon, back in Y——, when some hoodlums had locked her and the head librarian in the stockroom and threatened to tear off all their clothes and stamp them to death if they didn't tell them where the smutty books were kept.

It terrified and excited her.

Then Angus staggered to his feet, kicked the tray out of the the way, and they both stumbled over the threshold, just in time to see Kent racing back in their direction.

"The elevator!" the baron yelled. "Get in, get in, get in!"

Angus immediately shoved her and Hazel inside, pushed the Hold button, and waited until Montana had squeezed in with him.

"Mind the knife," she cautioned when Hazel tried to turn around in her corner.

"Sorry."

"Damn!" Kent said then, grabbing the door before it closed. "The notebooks!" He leapt back into the hall and pointed. "You three go on. I'll catch up. Be careful—he's gone round the bend now and there's no telling what he'll do next. Watch out for the elbow!"

As soon as the door shut, the car shuddered, and Hazel began to thump the wall and tap her foot impatiently.

"Elbow?" Lizzy asked.

"Elbow," Hazel confirmed.

155

"Balls," Angus muttered.

"No, that was last night," Hazel reminded him.

Lizzy forgave with a tolerant smile his lapse into the coarse and coursing venue of military patois, then turned to the tarted-up constable and said, "But how are we going to find an elbow?"

"Beats me, love," Hazel said. "I don't play tennis."

Angus said nothing.

The elevator juddered.

"Oh my," said Lizzy, feeling suddenly dizzy. "I don't know if I can do this."

"You have to," her darling but mysterious ex-army hero told her gently. "If we don't stop that madman now, who knows what he'll do at the sacrifice tonight?"

"Probably kill a few tourists for practice," Hazel suggested professionally as she watched the numbers count down to "Lobby." "All those people out there, some of them so drunk they can't stand up, some of them so tired they can't stand up, who's to tell which are dead and which are just snoring?" She pointed her gleaming knife at the door. "In point of procedural fact, he could be waiting down there for us right now. It wouldn't take much actually—just stand ready at the door, wait for it to open, then blast us all." She shrugged and fluffed her hair. "Could be."

"He has a gun?" Lizzy said, nearly shrieking.

"I don't know."

"Then how can he blast us?"

"If he has a gun, he can."

"Then we'll . . . we'll be . . ."

Hazel nodded grimly.

Manfully Angus eased to the front of the car, each arm firmly pushing each lady behind him. Lizzy nearly swooned both in reverence for his courage and in anticipation that now, at last, the horror she had been avoiding all this time would come home to roost with lots of blood and visible bones and cracked skulls and my God, woman, wake up and smell the lily pads! These are people you're thinking about, not some stupid book where giant fungi tromp all over London.

This, girl, is real life!

The car stopped.

She heard Hazel stropping her blade on her wrist.

She heard Angus pound a ready fist into his palm.

The door opened.

The Sergeant Major immediately leapt out with a blood curdling scream that dropped Reg, the night porter, over his counter.

There was no attack.

"The street!" he cried.

Lizzy glanced around for sight of Kent Montana, but the lobby was fairly empty except for the people wondering what all the shouting was about.

"Later, Liz," Angus told her as he grabbed her arm. "We've no time to lose. He'll catch up."

They ran to the entrance and gathered under the marquee. By the befuddled, bewildered, and here and there terrified expressions on some of the pedestrians, it was clear that the fleeing elbow had gone to the right.

" Some festival this is going to be," Angus muttered, "what with all the promised carnage and all."

"Unforgettable," Lizzy said with a shudder.

"Yes, that too."

"Right!" Angus snapped then. "Move out, my lovelies, three abreast, sharply now, and don't hesitate if you think you've found him."

There was no time for discussion. Hazel and her blade took the outside, Angus and his great fists the center, and Lizzy the inside, wishing she had brought better shoes to run in. Nevertheless, she managed to keep up, warily checking the doorways and storefronts, stoops and lighted lobbies. Her head still rang a little from its collision with the wall, but never had her senses been so alert, so finely tuned, so ready for danger.

It was definitely more stimulating than sending out late charges.

At the grocery, she poked her head in and out quickly, shivering at the slobbering sound the woman behind the counter made at her. Unless it was the bulldog perched in her lap.

At Rains Lane, she grabbed Angus' elbow and clung close, shuddering.

At the Druid's Cape Restaurant and Wine Grill, she stood on tiptoe to peer through the windows, seeing nothing but a couple of Americans who appeared to be arguing over their bill.

Progress was slow.

Not only did they have to watch the air for unusual displacements, they also had to be sure every reasonably elbow-size area was thoroughly checked, and her frustration level soon increased to the point where, when she spotted a cricket ball lying at the base of a wall and recalled Hazel's harrowing description of her encounter in the grocery, she screamed and kicked the hell out of it.

Angus patted her on the back.

She smiled sheepishly and took the lead as they hurried past the Bloodstone Casino and Clam Bar, from whose depths came the sounds of greedy slurping and card slapping.

Hazel fended off eight potential customers, and a uniformed constable who wanted to know when the hell she was going to show up for her shift, didn't she realize there was a Festival going on? Hazel only fluffed her hair and whispered something that Lizzy could only imagine; and when she did, her cheeks flushed as furiously as the other cop's.

"Damn," Angus muttered when they reached the next corner, "I hope the bastard doesn't take the tube."

"He can't," Lizzy advised. "He has no money."

"Don't need none, does he, darlin'? Can't see him to stop him jumping the queue."

She nodded. "Then be glad there is no Underground here."

"Damn, but you're quick."

She blushed.

"Oh nuts!" she said then.

Hazel snapped out her blade, and Angus whirled, fists at the ready. "What is it, darlin'?"

"We forgot the shaving cream."

"No matter, no matter. Seems like we don't need it anyhow."

A few disheartening minutes later, she felt the evening begin to settle over the peaked roofs of the village. The sky darkened, the streets grew more crowded, neon flared and music blared, and when they reached the park without a smidgen of success except for her shredding of a salami in a shop window, they realized that their man had given them the slip.

The crowds moved toward the park.

Several dozen gaily attired Druids marched down the center of the High Street in quick time to the beat of a goatskin drum stylishly handled by the headmaster of Merkleton Vo-Tech. In their midst, on a large slab of wood painted to resemble slate which rested on the shoulders of the largest of the men, was a black-haired woman in a skimpy white sacrificial costume. She laughed and tossed rose petals at the crowd, who laughed back and tossed coins at her.

Lizzy watched the procession, watched the woman fend off a few eager Druids and a kid with a zoom lens, then sagged against a lamppost with a despairing sigh. "It's too late. We've lost him. Oh dear, we've lost him."

"Yeah," agreed Hazel, "I think you're right." She popped the blade back into her purse and leaned over to rub her ankles. "And where is Kent? He should have been here by now."

"Oh, Angus!" Lizzy exclaimed, and began to run.

Back toward the Bowlingham.

Feeling that a dire, if not fatal error had been made.

After retucking her gun back in its place, Janice carried the unconscious Bowlingham cashier down to the lobby, where she nearly collided with an obviously plastered purple Druid. The Druid muttered an apology and staggered into an elevator; Janice glared at him, wondering where chivalry had gone that he hadn't offered to assist her with her burden, then squared her shoulders and lugged the woman into the bar, where she dropped her into the colonel's rather surprised lap.

"There's trouble," she said, flashing her badge.

The colonel gaped.

"Take care of her. She was nearly killed."

The colonel's monocle popped onto Petula's chest, and she stirred.

"You might want to call the police."

"But you are the police," the colonel said.

"Yes, but I'm only one of the police. I think, Colonel Braithe, we're going to need more of the police before this night is done."

Petula stirred.

The colonel glanced down. "Yes, yes, of course. Right away. I'll—right away."

Sure, she thought, and puffed back into the lobby, realized that the others must have already pursued the maniac into the street, and ran out to assist them. But they were gone, leaving in their wake a number of annoyed pedestrians rubbing their elbows and threatening to write their MPs in the morning.

She took a step to the left, a step to the right, and collided with a fat man in a vicuna coat, who excused himself hastily and ducked into the hotel, quite obviously on his way to some Druidic banquet or other. She glared at him, and his companion, whom she hadn't seen because of his bulk and her lack of it, and rubbed her hands as she pondered her next move.

Clearly Angus was on some trail or other.

Yet Dargren was invisible, so that trail was also obviously rather difficult to follow.

Kent was probably with them.

Another step left, another step right, and she spotted the final Red Moon Festival procession making its raucous, yet solemn way toward the park, and the Ringstones beyond. She suspected at that moment that her companions in terror had not, and would not, find Racig Dargren now.

There was no question, then, that the wisest course would be to head for the park herself. If the others had indeed failed to find the Welsh Vagabond by now, he would surely make good on his threat to show up, as it were, at the celebration.

Which, she noted as she dashed across the street through a break in the traffic, was due to begin in less than two hours.

Two hours.

Before Hell came to Merkleton.

·3·

The procession banged and hummed its ancient way through the gates.

The streets slowly emptied.

The shops and restaurants locked their doors and snapped off their lights.

A breeze rippled the banners that stretched across the High Street, snapping them once in a while, belling them like sails, letting them sag.

Scraps of paper scuttled along the gutters, and a flurry of dead leaves raced over the pavement.

For a moment, just for a moment, Merkleton was silent, and dark, and very, very still.

Then the moon tore away from a silver-edged cloud, and a prowling cat arched its back and hissed at an elbow leaning nonchalantly against the park's iron fence. The cat fled, howling, and invisible eyes peered through the trees and across the expanses of still green grass, down to the River George, flowing darkly through till morning.

There were lights down there on the Green, glaring white ones that marked the path along the riverbank, and bobbling gold ones that traced the Druid procession toward the Ringstones in the grove; flashbulbs flashed; voices murmured softly; someone banged a drum slowly; and Gretchen Wain giggled.

The elbow shook with anticipation.

And when a voice hummed an old country tune, a nightbird fled from its roost into the dark, a black tail feather spiraling gently to the ground.

✦ 4 ✦

The procession banged and hummed its ancient way through the gates.

The streets slowly emptied.

The shops and restaurants locked their doors and snapped off their lights.

A breeze rippled the banners that stretched across the High Street, snapping them once in a while, belling them like sails, letting them sag.

Scraps of paper scuttled along the gutters, and a flurry of dead leaves raced over the pavement.

For a moment, just for a moment, Merkleton was silent, and dark, and very, very still.

And Milo Yonker stood apprehensively in the elevator on his way up to the second-from-last floor. He kept his hood in place, his head down, his hands hidden in his voluminous sleeves, and he prayed that the woman carrying the other woman wouldn't come back and demand to know why he hadn't helped her.

It had been a close call; gallantry among fish 'n' chips shop owners was legendary in these parts, and he had actually come close to hyperventilating before deciding that his future was more important than playing Conan the Druid.

And his life, as well, which wouldn't be worth a penny farthing if Kirkie caught him trying to double-cross her.

He patted his chest to be sure the gun was still in his jacket, checked to make sure the cosh was still in his hip pocket, and checked the gold-trimmed hem to be sure the lock-picking tools were still in their secret pocket.

The elevator stopped.

He stepped into the silent hallway and made his way to the right, to the fire-exit stairwell, where he took off his shoes, threw back his hood, and crept up to the top landing. There he put his shoes back on, his hood back on, and pulled the heavy steel door toward him.

It didn't budge.

He panicked.

He pushed.

The door opened, and he leapt into the hall.

It was empty.

Silent.

He eased along the wall until he was opposite the door to Kent Montana's room.

Though he couldn't be positive, he was fairly sure that his lordship was in the room. He had seen the baron's friends pelt out of the hotel, but not the baron himself. Which was all right with him. Just a quick in-and-out, hands up, your lordship, don't mind me, just hand over the bloody notebooks, and he would be gone. Up the street like a bat out of hell, a bullet from a gun, an arrow from its bow. A shortcut once he passed the park, and he'd be at the sacrificial ceremonial grounds before anyone knew he'd been missing.

There, before Kirkie had a chance to announce that Milo's throat had seized up, he couldn't sing, and she hoped no one minded if they got straight on with the sacrifice, he would stun both her and them with a performance that would forever alter the course of his life.

He didn't think the audience would mind.

Kirkie, though, would demand an explanation before she killed him, the only part of the plan he hadn't quite worked out yet.

But it was too late now, baby; the fat was in the fire and the horn had sounded—it was time to get his due and get the hell out of town.

A slow, steadying deep breath, and he stepped cautiously up to the door, pressed his ear against it for several minutes, then took hold of the knob.

For purposes of concealment, and having already once tried to ride in the regular Bowlingham elevators, much to the chagrin of the other passengers and a damned poodle, Claudius chose the service elevator to take him to his destiny. Poetra rose beside him, sucking on her holder.

"Do you think we can eat after this?" she complained.

"I think we'll be too busy for the nonce, my dear."

She stamped her foot. "You promised!"

His smile, as cold as the elevator's polished steel walls, silenced her immediately, and he was able to concentrate more fully on the next stage of his plan.

Much of it depended upon that idiot, Yonker, mesmerizing the crowd with whatever garish and talentless performance the fishy little weasel had planned; with the audience—meaning nine tenths of the town and just about all the coppers—rapt or disgusted, it didn't matter which, he would nick his share of the Festival receipts, and a few quid over for expenses, and hop the next train down to London. By the time anyone had figured anything out, he would be at the Savoy, bribing everyone in sight to pretend he wasn't there.

It was perfect.

The elevator stopped.

No one would be able to stop him.

Perfect.

The door slid open.

"You want me to wait here?" Poetra asked.

He took her elbow and eased her into the hall, and together they hurried to the corner, rounded it . . .

And stopped.

"Well, boy!" Poetra pouted.

Claudius just barely stopped himself from tumbling into a plebeian gape.

There, up the hallway, bending over the door Claudius knew belonged to Kent Montana, was the purple Druid.

There was a moment of indecision, a moment of rage, a moment to clamp a hand over Poetra's mouth before she called out, and he hurried on, moving as quietly as he could, keeping close to the wall in case the Druid looked up. He had no idea who that ugly little creature was, nor why he was snooping around the baron's room. It didn't matter. He would have to be disposed of. Loose ends did not belong in the repertoire of a potential world conqueror.

The Druid turned the knob.

Claudius wrinkled his nose.

"My god!" he exclaimed involuntarily. "Jesus H. Yonker, is that you?"

Startled into a yelp and a hasty leap backward, the Druid spun around, threw back his hood, and said, "G'damn, Cana, what the hell are you doing here?"

Claudius opened his mouth and closed it.

Poetra waved her holder in regal disdain. "We're checking to make sure everyone who is supposed to be at the ceremony is at the ceremony, you smelly little person." She hip-waggled over to him and poked his chest with the ivory. "And you, you poop, are supposed to be there, singing or something."

"That's right," Claudius said, swearing silently to give his woman anything she wanted when this was over, even France. "Now, suppose you explain yourself."

Milo drew himself up. "I don't have to. I'm not on for another hour."

Claudius narrowed his eyes. "My boy, you're not on at all."

Then the door opened.

Milo immediately whipped out his gun, Claudius aimed his wolf's-head cane, and Poetra made threatening gestures with her holder.

"Well," Kent said. "Well."

There was no time to slam the door, sprint the five steps to the other side of the room, throw open the sash, and throw himself out the window in hopes of landing on someone soft, so Kent backed away and watched as the trio crowded in after him. He suspected, by the way they kept aiming their weapons at each other as well as him, that they weren't on the same side. He also suspected that, no matter which side they were on, none of them were on his.

"I want Dargren's notebooks, Montana," Claudius said. "Hand them over and there'll be no trouble."

"There will be if you give them to him," Milo warned. He peered at the books still lying on the desk. "Just dump them in a bag or something and toss 'em over."

"You toss them over to him," Claudius said, "and your head will have a rather fatal dent in it."

"You don't hand them over," Milo said, "and your chest will have a fatal hole in it."

"And what are you going to do?" Kent asked Poetra. "Smoke me to death?"

Poetra paled.

Kent thought he saw a ghost.

"The notebooks!" Claudius snapped.

"Here!" Milo ordered.

Kent picked them up, stacked them neatly, and wondered how long he would be able to string this out before Janice and the others realized he wasn't with them and would come back to get him and thus save his life. Unless, he thought, they had reckoned that Dargren would continue his relentless campaign of terror at the ceremony and that Kent, seeing they weren't waiting for him in the lobby, would join them there.

In which case, his ass was grass.

On the other hand, if he stalled, he lived longer automatically, even if his friends weren't coming to his rescue and his gun was in his pocket where he couldn't get at it with sufficient speed to prevent the Druid from shooting and the fat man from clubbing him first.

So thinking, and wishing he hadn't, he slipped his free hand into the other pocket and pulled out a cigarette lighter. Before anyone could stop him, he simultaneously flicked it open and lighted it.

And held the flame close to the notebooks.

"One move and they're ashes," he warned.

"Don't be stupid," Milo said in disgust. "They won't burn fast enough."

"Dare you take the chance?" he asked guilelessly. "Can you be sure that you can get me before I leap into the bathroom, lock the door behind me, and burn these things in the tub?"

Poetra climbed across the bed and closed the bathroom door. "Yes," she said.

"Can you take that chance?" he repeated seductively.

Milo licked his lips nervously; Claudius didn't dare because he knew he slobbered when he did.

"Mexican standoff," Kent declared.

Milo blinked.

"Movie term," Claudius told him.

Milo looked at his watch.

Kent sensed a timely necessity. "Just why," he said, "do you want these old things anyway?"

"Don't play us for fools," Claudius snapped angrily. "We know what's in them, and I want them. Now!"

Kent glanced down innocently. "What's in them?" He looked up. "You know?"

"Of course!" Milo said, nearly yelling. "Gretchen spilled the beans, you royalist pig and a Scot to boot. And *I need those damned songs*!"

"Songs?" Kent said. What in god's name was this idiot talking about?

"You are trying my patience," Claudius said. "And I need those damned songs more than he does." He snorted. "At least I know I can't sing."

"Oh, you're not that bad, Claudius," Poetra said.

"Songs?"

"And I suppose," Milo sneered, "you're going to sell them, right, Cana? Make a fortune and try to conquer the bloody world or something."

Claudius reeled from the blatant exposure of his plan. He recovered swiftly, however, and said, "And I suppose you're going to learn a couple between now and the time you're supposed to go on, and pray that you'll become the . . . the what? The Fish Chips Vagabond?"

Milo gasped.

Poetra laughed cruelly.

Kent looked at the notebooks, looked at each of the antagonists in turn, and realized that none of them had the faintest idea what had been happening in Merkleton over the past forty-eight hours. He also realized that handing over the notebooks, even if he divided them between these idiots, would mean the imminent, if not immediate, end of his life.

Unfortunately a dash for the door, in this small room, was next to impossible, even if Milo didn't shoot him and Poetra didn't stab him. Claudius Cana himself only had to take a deep breath to block his escape.

Now what, he wondered, would a butler do in a situation like this?

"We are at an impasse," Claudius announced.

"Too right," Milo grumbled.

"Therefore, I suggest a temporary combination of forces, just long enough for us to gain those notebooks without harm. Once that is accomplished, we can surely work out our differences like true Englishmen."

"I have a gun," the Druid reminded him.

"As I said," Claudius said with a slight nod.

It was then that Kent realized that holding a lighted lighter entailed several inherent dangers—the fluid, for one, was bound to run out, and for another, the thing was growing damned hot. Soon it would be too hot to handle.

"Look," he said.

Claudius did, quickly, the walking stick carving a slow menacing arc in the air between Yonker and the baron.

"I feel," Kent continued, "that I must warn you that what you're looking for isn't here."

"Sure it is," the Druid said. "You're holding them."

"Well, yes, I am, but they're not what you want."

"*Au contraire,*" contradicted Claudius continentally. "They are exactly what I want."

"Perhaps," Kent persisted, "if I read—"

Milo's finger tightened on his trigger; Cana's hand tightened on his cane; Poetra's holder puffed ominously.

Damn, Kent thought; I'm going to have to pray for a miracle.

Someone knocked on the door.

He grinned.

"Don't answer it!" Milo and Claudius ordered in unison.

"Your lordship?" a muffled voice called from the corridor.

Kent's grin softened to a smile. "Gentlemen, if I don't answer, whoever's out there will think something's wrong, call the manager, and . . ." He sighed.

Milo checked his watch.

"Your lordship, are you all right?"

Poetra said, "Answer it. We will be watching. One false move and you're a dead peer."

Nodding his agreement, Kent maneuvered around Cana and made to open the door. Then he reached onto the wardrobe shelf and pulled down a white plastic bag which was, in calmer times, used to carry laundry down to Reg, for washing. He dumped the notebooks in; he took a deep breath; he opened the door.

"Your lordship," said Zero Zuller with a deferential smile, "I was just on my way to the ceremony and all, and I was wondering if you were going to bring my new accordion with you."

Kent thanked the gods, the elevators, and the carpeting for his good fortune.

"Damn me," spat Cana, "the man's blind!"

At which point Kent sprang out of the room, yanked the

door to, and grabbed Zero's arm. Seconds later, to the sound of much stumbling and cursing in the room behind him, he dragged the blind man toward the stairwell, since, he noted, the elevator door had already closed.

"M'lord!" Zuller protested.

"Don't talk," Kent said. "Run! There are people trying to kill me."

"I shouldn't wonder," the blind man muttered, "you dragging folks around like this all the time."

Nevertheless, Zuller plunged ahead of him, taking the metal-tipped steps two at a time, one hand burning along the railing, the other clamped to his white cashmere cap.

Kent followed nearly as rapidly. His only hope was to get to the Green before the others caught up. There, he could mingle with the crowd until he found his partners, apprise them of this new complication, and hope against hope that everyone would kill everyone off and leave him out of it.

But, he thought as he lunged into the lobby behind Zuller, one miracle a night is more than any sane man could expect.

Once outside, the blind man veered to the left. Kent grabbed his coat collar and steered him back in the right direction.

"Thanks," Zero said.

"Don't mention it."

They ran.

Through the deserted streets.

Through the park gates.

Down the slope toward the river, where he saw hundreds of people gathered along the riverbank path, all of them moving slowly but with great jocularity toward the oak grove on the bluff.

Zero ran on.

Kent slowed.

It all comes to this, he thought grimly; God help us, it all comes to this.

~VIII~

The Revenge

◆ 1 ◆

The Merkleton Ringstones were not unique.

But they were pretty impressive.

They were large blocks of time-encrusted granite standing ten feet high, nine of them rough-hewn and arranged in an irregular wide circle thirty yards in diameter. In the center, a horizontal stone nine feet long and three feet tall rested on a low mound of grassy earth; atop that was yet another horizontal stone overhanging its ancient base by several inches all around. In the center of this, the Sacrificial Slab, were gashes and runnels and channels stained dark with either the dried blood of long-dead virgins, or several hundred years of dust and grime. The debate rages.

The ground itself held low grass and brown weeds that whispered when the breeze blew up from the river.

And the bluff upon which all this stood was a full forty feet above the River George. A forty-foot drop with no obstruction, no rocks for climbing or handholds, no worn lovers' path down to the curative mud flats and the river. Those passing on their boats saw nothing of what lay inside the wall of trees; those walking seldom bothered to get this far because of the wall of trees the path vanished into; and those who did venture to the stones did not stay long.

Even in daylight, the clearing was inhospitable.

Except on the night of the Red Moon Festival.

For outside the ring, between the awesome stones themselves and the first of the full-boled oaks which were rumored to have been planted during the reign of Queen Anne, was yet another ring, this of cleverly erected wooden bleachers which somehow, thanks to the artistry of local tradesmen, managed not to be intrusive while, at the same time, providing all with a good view of the Slab, unless, of course, you were on the lower seats stuck behind a Ringstone.

Small spotlights had been rigged in the trees to illuminate the prehistoric stage in such a way that made the granite appear to glow from within.

There were no banners here, no pennants, no flags.

There were only the stones and their shadows.

The dark sky without the blemish of a star served as an appropriate roof.

The trees blocked all lights from Merkleton itself.

And the silence—itself dark and foreboding, and maintained as the first of the audience reached the grove. No one spoke; there were only a few hesitant whispers, and the music of the Druids back on the Green faded and was gone.

Expectant, then, was the mood as the Festival neared its climax.

There would be the usual speeches of brief duration, the music which had launched more than one artist on a reasonably successful career, and the sacrifice itself of a woman in a skimpy white sacrificial costume, after which there would be refreshment and sweets back down on the Green, and more parties than the bluenoses could shake a stick and a cop at.

Expectant.

Hushed.

While the Ringstones waited for the end to begin.

·2·

Midway down the Green path, Kent slowed to a walk and watched as hysterical Zero raced on, swinging his arms wildly and screaming a warning. Obligingly people got out of his way, which led him soon after to one of the docks off which he air-sprinted for several yards before sinking into the river. Immediately, several onlookers were in the water with him, dragging him to the riverbank, where they emptied his lungs, fussed about his handicap, and pressed several flagons of lager into his eager hands.

It was clear no one believed his story of danger from a self-made tailor or an invisible man.

Kent hefted the white bag and moved on, aware that time ticked against him, yet helpless to do anything about it.

Where the hell are you, he asked the Welsh Vagabond; where the hell are you?

To his right he could see the boisterous crowd moving slowly toward the grove, Druids and civilians, teens and children, massing for the ceremony. Laughter and music combined to fill the air; impromptu dancing and a few drunken fights; the woman in the skimpy white sacrificial costume surrounded by her eager entourage; and down on the riverbank, Janice Plase and the others, looking dishearteningly dispirited.

So much, he thought, for the other miracle.

They spotted him just as he reached the lower path, and he didn't have to ask for the results of their pursuit; their greetings told him all he needed to know. So he told them about Cana and the purple Druid, how his escape had been engineered by Zero, and how he feared that carnage would be the watchword for the evening.

"Songs?" Lizzy said incredulously. "They thought those books had songs?"

"Sounds reasonable to me," Angus told her. "He was a singer, you know."

"I suppose." She shrugged. "How were they to know that the idiot's a scientific genius, far ahead of his time?"

"They weren't to know," the sergeant major agreed.

"What difference does it make?" Kent groused. "I've nearly been killed a couple of times tonight, and we're still no closer to saving any of those poor people. Or me, if it comes to that, which it damn well better not."

Hazel was propositioned by several bikers, who weren't put off in the least when she showed them her badge; they doubled their offer.

"Maybe," Janice offered, "the colonel called the station. Then we'd have more help."

Kent doubted it would do any good. "A thousand coppers aren't going to uncover what they can't see." He looked out over the water. "No, we can't depend on the police to help us."

"Well, thank you very much," Janice huffed.

"I didn't mean that."

"I know that, but I felt obligated."

"Besides, do you think Easewater would believe our story?" She pointed. "You have the notebooks."

"He'd think they were fakes."

"Don't forget poor Mary."

"Aye, but no proof an invisible man did that."

"What about the cashier at the hotel? And me? And the others? We saw him, remember? On the piecemeal side, admittedly, but we all did see him."

He pondered; he speculated; he thought; he considered.

Janice looked pointedly at her watch.

Hazel had the bikers up to triple what her fee would have been had she been what she looked like. When they protested, she stroked the fox with the ermine trim and told them she had appearances to keep.

"No time," he decided at last. "The only thing we can do is split up and hope for a mistake on his part. He is crazy, after all." A glance at the crowd, and he shook his head wearily. "On the other hand, he may already be up there."

"Then let's get moving," Angus declared with a decisive

clap of his meaty hands. "All this standing about and thinking out loud is doing us no good. We spread out, we search, we get to the grove and we position ourselves." He raised an eyebrow. "Naught else we can do now."

Janice agreed.

Hazel agreed and shooed the bikers away.

Lizzy said that if they couldn't see what they were looking for, especially since she'd forgotten the shaving cream, maybe there was something else they could do to avoid a great deal of frustration and agonizing.

"Like what?" Kent asked.

She nodded toward a toddler Druid.

Kent frowned.

Janice frowned.

Hazel didn't think a kid in a bathrobe would do them a damn bit of good.

Until Lizzy said, "The sacrifice."

"Wrong," Kent said.

"Yes!" Janice cried, and shooed the bikers away again.

Angus replaced his cap and scratched it.

Kent wondered if the librarian was a long-lost cousin, on his mother's goddamn side.

But when it was evident they were going to gang up on him again, plant him in the center of yet another plan to paint a figurative target on his forehead, he decided that he might as well take charge and get in as many safeguards as he could before he died.

"All right," he said. "All right. But I'm not wearing any skimpy white sacrificial gown."

Lizzy's expression expressed her disappointment.

"Well, for heaven's sake, woman," he said, "I'm not a virgin, you know."

"Neither is she, I'll wager," said Angus, pointing to the woman just now vanishing into the oak grove with her faithful Druid bearers.

Kent smiled stiffly and stepped up to the path. He walked briskly, partly in order to catch up with the laggers, partly to avoid giving himself too much time to think about the idiocy on which he was about to embark.

Yet it was their only chance.

And before they were halfway to the grove, Hazel and Janice

were dispatched ahead, to negotiate, cajole, or threaten, if need be.

Lizzy expressed admiration for the baron's courage; Angus gave him a hearty slap on the back.

Kent just watched the slope, the path behind him, the path ahead of him, the riverbank, the boats bobbing at the docks, and anything else he could look at. The others were so excited, he didn't bother to tell them that if Dargren had been nearby, with them none the wiser, this whole thing was going to hell in a handbasket.

"You know," Angus said quietly, dropping back to walk beside him, "it's occurred to me that the invisible bugger might have overheard us."

Kent ignored him.

"And if he didn't, sir, he might well be watching our every step. Well, your every step."

Kent sped up just a little.

"But I'm glad you're not going to wear the skimpy white sacrificial gown. You are nobility, you know. There are limits."

"Thank you."

Angus tipped his cap. "Don't mention it, sir. My pleasure."

The procession vanished into the dark mouth of the grove.

Hazel and Janice returned with an armful of Druidic robes. Kent didn't ask how their costumes had been obtained, though he did note that Hazel's hair was no longer carefully fluffed. He only hoped the defrocked Druids had gotten their robes' worth.

Moments later, under cover of the trees, they were all dressed in the exotic attire of the evening.

"Now remember," he said as they made their way back to the path, "with these things on we'll be able to stand inside the Ringstones. We must keep together, but not right next to each other. And we must keep our eyes sharp, our wits about us, and just do whatever the others do so we won't be spotted."

"Well, I'm certainly not sacrificing any virgin," Janice said stiffly.

"You won't have to," he told her.

"Well, just so you know."

He nodded.

"God," Angus said then, "it's bloody warm under all this."

His robe was black; he looked like a monk eager for the Inquisition. "Should've left me shirt behind."

Janice looked at him.

"You'll get used to it," Lizzy assured him. "At least I had the sense to leave that tatty coat, even if it was a present from my mother."

Janice looked at her.

Hazel adjusted her hood. "Just up ahead, lads," she said. "God, I'm frying in here. You wouldn't think a goddamn tight skirt would be so bloody warm, would you?"

Janice looked at her.

Kent rolled his shoulders, plucked up his hood, and after a moment's hysterical and silent screaming that he was too young to die and too old to put up with all this crap, was the first to step into the clearing. Into the light. In full view of several hundred townsfolk and tourists just waiting for the lid to blow off so they could get on with it. He took a slow series of deep breaths that didn't calm him a bit as he listened to the murmuring of the crowd in the bleachers, the muffled tap of the drum, the shuffling of feet as the procession made its way to the Sacrificial Slab.

Janice tugged at his sleeve.

He looked down and smiled. "It'll be all right," he said. "What the hell, we can't turn around now."

"Kent?"

He leaned closer, smelled her skin, saw her eyes, saw those lips.

"Do you still have your clothes on under there?"

Claudius made it as far as the park fountain before he had to stop. The moment his buttocks hit the nearest stone bench with a rather embarrassing flop, he resolved to begin a rigorous diet the very day—nay, the very second—he had finished conquering the world. A plan which, though delayed, was not yet ready to be jettisoned. All he had to do was locate that arrogant Scots baron, tear off his head, and grab the notebooks before the weasel did. He hadn't been defeated; he was only going to be a couple of hours later than he thought.

Poetra stood before him, one foot tapping impatiently.

"My dear," he said, mopping his face with one end of his fringed white scarf, "not to worry."

"I'm not worried," she said. "I'm hungry."

"Later."

Petulantly she sighed and peered down the path. "That ugly Druid person isn't around."

The fat man nodded. "I can see that."

"Do you think I should go on? Maybe I can find him."

"And what would you do if you did?"

"Oh, Claudius, how do I know? Seduce him, I reckon, and enlist him in our cause until we don't need him anymore. Then drown him or something. I guess. Maybe. How should I know? I'm too hungry to think straight."

Despite his heavy breathing, and the perspiration beading like bowling balls on his florid face, he beamed. "You are amazing, my pet."

"I suppose," she answered disinterestedly. "But I tell you this, Claudius—once I've done my bit, I'm going to be fed or you can conquer the soddin' world on your own."

He didn't care. He waved her away. Some peace without whining might enable him to think more clearly, develop contingency plans just in case, God forbid, he wasn't able to get hold of Montana.

Conquering Merkleton and the world ought not to depend on a single score.

Poetra kissed him coldly on the forehead, wiped her lips quickly, and tottered on, muttering to herself and waving her holder, and soon disappeared into the black.

Once she was gone, the clatter of her heels swallowed by the trees and bushes, he shook himself.

As the perspiration cooled, he looked over his shoulder at the deserted street.

As the blood pounding in his ears finally subsided, he listened to the silence.

And he stiffened when he heard:

"When I hear you a-calling 'cross the moors, my darlin',
"And I throw another hunk of peat on the flame—"

Claudius scowled, his head swiveling as best it could on such a neck to catch the person interrupting his cogitations.

His scowl deepened.

There was no one here but him.

But that voice sounded as if the singer were standing right in front of him.

"—I know that you've come back with love for me, darlin',
"Because Bristol done turned its heartless back on you—"

No.

Now it was on his left.

"*So listen, my sweet, as I sing you this song—*"

No, wrong again.

It was on his right.

"*The peat-fire blues, pure as my love is long.*"

He began to sweat.

Impossible.

My God, he knew that voice!

Impossible.

"Who's there?" he demanded, furious that his voice did not sound all that world-conquering.

Someone laughed.

"I said, who's there?"

Someone moaned, loudly.

He rumbled to his feet and brandished the cane. "Yonker, is that you? Damnit, man, show yourself!"

"*The peat-fire blues—*"

He backed away from the fountain. "I know it's you, you weasel. And I am not enjoying your little game."

"*Pure smokin' proof of my heart's burnin' for you.*"

Claudius laughed . . . nervously. "My lord, man, is that the best you can do? Imitating the greatest singer on the face of this planet?" He laughed again, scornfully. "They'll bury you, Yonker. You'll never get away with it."

"Oh yes, I will," a voice said in his ear.

He spun around.

There was no one there.

A breeze blew across the fountain then, ruffling the ends of his scarf, though he didn't feel it on his face.

"Yonker!"

He gaped at his chest—the breeze had moved the scarf until it had crossed over his heart. Then he looked farther down and saw the kneecap.

"Yonker!" he screamed.

"Wrong," the voice whispered, and Claudius gasped when his cane was yanked from his grasp and flung across the concrete.

"It can't be," he sputtered. "You're dead. The police, whom I called in Y——, killed you. You . . . you're dead!"

"No, I'm not," he was contradicted. "And don't think I

didn't see you, in Y——, that summer. Don't think I don't know what you're after."

"Dead," Cana gasped, his knees trembling, his waist rolling, his buttocks tightening, his chins aflutter.

"Wrong again," said Racig Dargren, and the kneecap blurred as the ends of the scarf flew over Cana's shoulders, and the white satin tightened around the fat man's fat throat.

There were some three dozen Druids around the Slab now, in two concentric circles. Their robes described all the colors of the spectrum, foreign and domestic, all their faces were hidden, all their hands slipped into their sleeves. Quickly Kent and his companions elbowed and shouldered their determined but courteous way into the outer circle, where he spied the clever manner in which Merkleton electricians had run their wires underground in order to feed power to the camouflaged microphones on the top portion of the Slab.

The first speaker of the evening stepped out of the circle onto a raised stone platform behind the Slab.

Kent relaxed; it wasn't Dargren who threw back an olive hood in a theatrical gesture and rattled a sheath of papers evidently containing greetings, remarks, and spontaneous political jokes. So he took the opportunity to study the shadowed visages of those nearest him, soon grateful to be able to cross off more than ten from his list of possible madmen. Fifteen Druids to his left, he could see Angus doing the same as well, and seventeen to his right, Hazel was using her policewoman's guile to fathom hithertofore unknown identities; Janice had remained hard at his side.

"See anyone?" he whispered from the side of his mouth.

A Druid hushed him with a gesture.

"I'm naked," she whispered back.

A Druid hushed her.

The speaker asked for a round of applause for Claudius Cana, the backbone, the leader, the organizer, the heart and soul of the Red Moon Festival.

The audience applauded and whistled.

The Druids stamped their feet.

"What do you mean, naked?"

The speaker introduced another speaker, a freckle-faced woman in a blue and brown robe, who apologized for the nonappearance of the traditional Druid singer, but acknowl-

edged that he still might show up if he knew what was good
for him.

Gretchen, who lay prone on the Slab and bound by leather
straps for authenticity, was thought by some to be fast asleep.

The woman asked for volunteers.

"I thought you'd all taken your clothes off so you could
wear this dumb costume without frying."

There were no takers. Too many recalled too vividly how
Racig Dargren, the Welsh Vagabond, had ruined this night for
too many others by bursting upon the scene with the first of
his string of mega–country hits.

The first speaker returned to calm the crowd, which had
begun to exhibit signs of sacrificial withdrawal.

"Are you crazy? It's cold out here."

"Don't I bloody know it."

A Druid hushed them both.

Kent suggested, in rusty Gaelic, what the Druid could do
with his hushing and his gestures.

Then the Druid with the drum ascended the platform and
began a hypnotic rhythm that soon quieted the crowd.

The sacrifice was imminent.

The outer circles of Druids began to shuffle to the right,
while the inner circle began to shuffle to the left.

Kent was forced to follow or be trampled; nevertheless, he
strained for a sign, a hint, a token of any untoward and un-
connected moving bodily part. Then a third good word la-
mentably unused by butlers popped to mind—frantic—when
two Druids in blinding white flanked the drummer.

The one on the left carried a massive bundle of mistletoe;
the one on the right carried a hell of a big knife.

Milo snaked and slithered along his shortcut as rapidly as
his robe allowed when it wasn't getting caught on twigs and
thorns and sticky things he couldn't see in the dark and didn't
want to know about.

He was late.

He was seriously out of breath.

And Kirkie was going to castrate him if he showed up without
the notebooks. The trouble was, she would castrate him anyway
when she learned that he'd had no intention of running away
and selling the Vagabond's songs in the first place, thus en-
abling them to live a life of languid luxury. But he couldn't

tell her that he had intended from the first to claim the songs as his own and sing his way to adulation and fortune. She was too jealous. If she couldn't have him, no one could, and certainly not millions of adoring fans of the female persuasion who, in all likelihood if the tabloids were to be believed, were all too willing to share their life experiences with a balladeer of his sensitive nature.

She'd kill him.

If the shortcut didn't do him in first.

He was confused.

But he was close.

There! Up ahead! The glow of the clearing, the crowd listening to the town council leader telling a joke about the Welshman, the Scotsman, and the Englishman rowing across the North Sea in an Irish boat with a Frenchman at the rudder and a Spaniard playing gin with a blind German. It was a stupid joke, and where the hell, he wanted to know, did the Hungarian come from?

Not that it mattered.

The audience didn't laugh.

The Druids didn't stamp their appreciative feet.

And he didn't have a clue how he was going to get out of this mess with all his bodily parts and functions intact.

He would have to do something drastic.

He would have to make a song up.

"Kick them cattle from here to Aberdeen—"

He froze.

"Ain't gonna use no ridin' machine—"

He fell against a tree and grabbed the bark. Then he blinked in confusion when he realized that the song, and the singer, weren't on the stone stage at all—they were somewhere behind him.

In the woods.

In the dark.

"My Shetland pony is all I need—"

No.

On his right.

"Fiddle in my hands—"

Oh Lord, no.

On his left.

"Gal on my knee—"

He leapt away from the tree, spun around, fell down, stood

up, and started to run for the clearing. He managed only a dozen yards before something tripped him and he plunged head-long into a bush whose branches tangled him as surely as if he'd been hogtied by an expert.

"*Haggis in my belly—*"

Milo began to whimper as he struggled to free himself.

"*And a couple of pounds in my pocket to make sure I can pay for all the damned food these ugly cattle are going to need before they get to market which is too far for any sane man to drive in the first place.*

"*But who cares?*

"*I'm free!*"

Milo crawled out of the bush and rocked back on his knees. "It's you, isn't it?" he whispered, half in fear, half in awe.

" 'Struth, it is," a voice whispered.

"I—"

"You wanted to steal my songs."

Milo shook his head violently. "God, no. I'd never do a thing like that."

"You lying to me, lad?"

"I swear I'm not!"

The voice laughed, and something large and heavy slammed on Milo's head. And in that last second before he became forever one with the black except where the clearing's glow was, he wondered how Kirkie was going to take this turn of events.

◆ 3 ◆

Kent sensed the moment was near when, as the drummer sounded his last thump, there was a slight commotion among the Druids on the far side of the Slab. Seconds later the drummer stepped down, the crowd hushed, and a purple-robed Druid stepped into the light. If Dargren was going to make his move, Kent knew it would be soon, and he intensified his efforts to locate the reasonably invisible man so that he could then work out a hasty plan to stop him without getting killed in his own right.

The lights dimmed.

The Druid with the mistletoe began to pass the branches over the body of the woman in the skimpy white sacrificial gown, at the same time keening an incantation that rose the hairs on the backs of the necks of everyone in the audience.

The drum sounded.

Gretchen stirred, fluttered her eyes, and smiled bravely.

The sprigs of mistletoe were arranged around her body, the last one placed gently across her forehead.

The lights dimmed.

The drum sounded.

The purple Druid took the sacrificial knife with its gold hilt and gleaming blade and stepped forward.

The deknifed Druid took over the keening from the Druid who used to have the mistletoe.

The drum sounded.

The other Druids dropped to their knees, leaving Kent momentarily exposed until he dropped as well, and yanked Janice down with him.

The audience rustled in expectation.

185

The drum sounded.

The purple Druid raised the knife over his head, shafts of light flaring from the blade into the eyes of the onlookers, who were duly impressed.

Suddenly Kent nudged Janice sharply and said, "Jesus Christ, it's him!"

Janice yelped. "What?"

He pointed. "Damnit, look!"

She did.

She gasped.

And he presumed she saw the deadly sacrificial knife being held high in the air. Floating in the air. Because the purple Druid's sleeves had fallen back, to reveal nothing but air where arms should have been.

"Let's go," he said, leaping to his feet.

"I can't," she whispered.

"Why the hell not?"

The drum sounded.

Gretchen began to scream.

"Because I'm naked, you ass, that's why not!"

"You are not! You have a robe on!"

"Oh," she said, and leapt to her feet.

The drum sounded.

Kent began to run.

The blade trembled.

Janice leapt over a Druid and charged the Slab.

The audience muttered, the assembled Druids growled.

The purple Druid shouted, "Revenge!"

The blade steadied, Gretchen screamed and thrashed at her bonds, the Druids staggered to their collective feet, the audience lunged to its collective feet because this wasn't the way the program book read, and someone somewhere blew hard on a whistle a few of the customers thought was feedback from the mikes.

In a prodigious leap that startled even him, Kent landed on his knees on the Slab, his hands up and grasping what he supposed and prayed like hell were Dargren's invisible wrists.

Gretchen writhed between them.

Dargren hissed, "Too late, you fool," and forced the blade down, ever downward, its razor-sharp point aiming straight for the sacrificial heart.

Kent grunted and forced the blade up.

Janice picked up a stone and shouted, "Hold it right there! This is the police!"

At that, all the Druids threw off their hoods, to reveal three dozen special agents led by none other than Inspector Easewater himself, looking none too shabby in a royal-blue robe.

Dargren's hood fell back.

Those who could see shrieked at the horrid sight of nothing to see.

The blade inched downward.

"I'm stronger than you," the Welsh Vagabond gloated. "I'm going to have my way at last."

The blade inched downward.

"And when I'm done with her, I'm going to cut out your liver."

The blade inched downward.

Kent, in order to gain more leverage, placed a knee on Gretchen's thigh and strained upward, lifting the blade away from its rippling target.

Pandemonium and panic flung the audience individually from its seats, which resulted in a lot of pushing and shoving and people falling under other people.

The police were helpless; Easewater himself made it clear when he bellowed that one minor distraction and his lordship would falter, the blade would do its work, and the girl would die.

Janice threw the rock away in frustration.

Angus caught Lizzy when she keeled over in a semi-conscious state.

"Die!" said the voice that came from the lips of a mouth Kent couldn't see.

He grunted, strained, and placed his other knee on Gretchen's thigh, hoisting the blade even higher.

Gretchen passed out.

Dargren chuckled madly.

Jesus, Kent thought, and felt his muscles reach the end of their endurance. They quivered; they strained; they began inexorably to weaken.

And inexorably the blade descended.

At that moment, Gretchen stopped screaming, the audience in its terror stopped running, and the silence that fell upon the clearing was broken only by the grunts of a man and a Druid robe locked in mortal combat.

Then, quite softly, from somewhere near the trees:

"*We shall meet in the coal mines,*

"*We shall gather in the Highlands—*"

Feverishly, inspired by a sudden thought as she witnessed the hellish impasse on the Slab, Janice fumbled with the leather straps that held the woman prisoner. When Angus saw her intent, he placed Lizzy reverently on the ground and dashed forward, working just as feverishly on the other side, all the while the two of them looking up at the men who struggled to the death above them.

Someone began clapping a fervent gospel beat.

"*We shall cross the River George in that sweet by-and-by.*"

The second the last of the straps had been loosened, Angus nodded.

Janice nodded.

They darted to the sacrificial woman's feet and, on the count of three, yanked her clear, thumping her head only once against the ridges of the bloody stone.

Kent, however, instantly found himself astonished, dismayed, and flat on his back because the thighs he'd been using for extra height had been taken from him, spilling him sideways, thence over, and soon done.

"Aha!" Dargren screamed.

Shit, Kent thought, and watched his hands quake as the knife pressed closer, closer, closer to the hollow of his throat.

Hazel, for it was she who had begun the famous tune, grabbed a microphone.

The clapping was picked up by the rest of the Druids.

"*We shall spread our jam on angels' scones,*

"*We shall take our tea in silver'd cups—*"

Herman Easewater, in a basso that filled the clearing, stood beside his constable, one hand around her waist, the other urging his lads on.

Kent felt the sweat begin to slip into his eyes, stinging them, blinding him. The blade swerved sideways and nicked his forearm, swerved again, and opened the flesh on his other arm. Blood welled and flowed. Dargren giggled.

"*We shall sup upon the River George in that sweet old by-and-by.*"

The drummer picked up the beat.

One of the Salvation Army band members yanked a tambourine from beneath his tunic. His comrades grabbed their instruments and threw aside their songbooks.

The audience gathered among the trees, the Ringstones, and soon found a harmony that made a number of them weep.

"I know what they're trying to do," Dargren said, the shifting of muscle and weight telling Kent that the man had climbed onto the Slab. "It won't work."

For a brief second, Kent Montana realized a morbid dream that few of the world's population hadn't entertained at one time or another—he was actually present at his own funeral.

"*O Lord, Lord, we shall soon stand with Asquith,*

"*We shall dance with good Queen Bess—*"

He lashed out with a leg, caught Dargren on what may or may not have been a hip, and flipped himself over, straddling the Invisible Man and feeling his lips pull away from his teeth in a decidedly unbaronial, feral grin.

"Now who's going to die, you tuneless wonder?" he snarled. "Now who's going to pay for the death of Mary Shweet?"

"*Lord, Lord, we shall follow the Bonnie Prince in that sweet old by-and-by.*"

Dargren's kneecap vanished and his teeth appeared, one of which was in serious need of attention.

"She . . . couldn't . . . sing," the Vagabond said.

Kent grunted at a knee slammed into his side.

"And . . . her . . . flowers . . . were . . . ugly!"

At that, Dargren wriggled a knee into Kent's stomach and thrust him up and back. Kent lost his grip and fell onto the Slab, dodged a swing of the knife, and only barely managed to grab hold of a forearm. Dargren kicked a shin; Kent butted the teeth, which vanished and were replaced, in its suitable position, by a navel of such bizarre convolution that he nearly stopped the fight just to stare. Then the singer's knee came too damn close to his groin, and he wrenched the arm up and over, wresting the man onto his back.

"*All our Mums and Dads,*

"*All the gals and lads—*"

Dargren, however, used his free hand to club Kent's ear, knocking him just off balance enough to reverse their positions and take another slice from Kent's right arm.

This time, however, the blade was sideways.

And it was less than an inch from Kent's exposed throat.

"*All shall cross the Rover George in that good old by-and-by.*"

"River," Dargren muttered as the blade touched Kent's flesh.

"What?"

"They said 'Rover.' It's 'River.'"

Kent swallowed and tried to force his throat to wrap itself around his spine. "Rover, you bastard," he gasped.

"River, you scum," Dargren sneered.

Kent, weakened by blood loss and the constant slamming against the Slab, marshaled the last of his strength and flung the Invisible Man upward without losing his grip in the physical sense. Now they were kneeling face-to-face whatever.

"Rover," he argued. "Every British school kid knows that."

"Well, goddamnit," Dargren snapped, "I wrote the song, I ought to know."

"*O Lord, Lord!*"

The navel winked out.

"Then you wrote it wrong."

Dargren hissed in indignation.

Realizing he wouldn't get another chance like this, Kent released one of his hands and smashed his fist into where he thought the man's teeth ought to be. They weren't there; but from the sound of it, his nose was.

Dargren groaned.

His hand released the blade, which skittered to the edge of the Slab and disappeared over the side.

"*Lord! Lord!*"

Dargren screamed in despair.

Kent bashed the fist into the nose again, except it was the man's teeth.

"*Across the River George in that sweet . . .*

"*Old . . .*

"*By . . .*

"*And . . .*

"*By . . . !*"

Dargren whipped a forearm across Kent's forehead, which, forewarned by a subtle shift in the air, ducked, thus sending the singer sprawling invisibly onto the stone. But before Kent could grab him, the man slithered away and leapt to the ground.

Kent followed.

It wasn't hard—the navel had been replaced, in somewhat dubious fashion, by Dargren's hard-driving buttocks.

Dargren barreled through the finger-snapping, howling, foot-stomping Druids, lunged into a gap in the bleachers, and dove into the trees.

Despite his stinging wounds, Kent managed to stay within a few yards of the fleeing maniac, determined that after all this, Dargren should not escape.

Then the trees fell away.

"O

"*Lord!*"

Racig Dargren screamed.

And Kent Montana stood panting on the edge of the bluff and watched the Welsh Vagabond plummet into the mudflats of the ever-flowing River George.

-IX-

Epilogue

◆ 1 ◆

Time moved rather slowly after that excitement.

Once Dargren had completed his final plunge to infamy, Kent was joined by his companions and representatives of the neo-Druidic constabulary as they made their way through the trees back to the riverbank and thence to the mud flats. It was easy to see where the mad singer had landed—the hole in the odoriferous mud marked his position, and his buns in the moonlight shone a ghastly pale. Within minutes, ambulances, nurses, and doctors arrived from Merkleton Mercy to care for those injured in the original panic, and to bind Kent's various slices and slashes; the bruises were left to fend for themselves.

Inspector Easewater stood with him as several constables waded across the flats to pull the Vagabond from his temporary grave and lay him on a stretcher. As they passed, the inspector stopped them and pulled the muddy sheet away from the man's face.

"Well, I'll be damned," said Angus.

They all stared in various states of amazement, the River George muttering beside them, the moon reflected in the running black water.

And Racig Dargren, once invisible most of the time, began to return to his visible state. A pore here, a freckle there, a strand of dark hair over on that side next to an ear. Seconds later, as they watched in combined horror and fascination, the transformation was complete.

Inspector Easewater slapped his notebook shut and said it for them all: "Jesus, he was an ugly son of a bitch."

Reports came in of bodies found in various places around and on the Green.

The Inspector excused himself, bowed, and waded into the official investigation with a flourish; Kent and the others, left in the vacuum created by the subsiding of their respective adrenaline rushes, climbed wearily up to the High Street and back to the hotel.

The Bowlingham, they soon discovered, hadn't seen such excitement since the end of the Great War. The residents' bar quickly overflowed into the lobby, the lobby swiftly overflowed into the street, and several Druid and C&W bands played wherever they could find the room.

Kent Montana and Janice Plase, still in their now somewhat disheveled robes, sat on Reg Olifer's night porter counter and watched the merrymakers sweep past them, listened to the ludicrously out-of-proportion gossip about the maniac at the ceremony, and were grateful that few stopped long enough for more than a quick hello.

"Are you all right?" she asked, patting his leg.

"I'll live," he said, though he wasn't at all sure it wasn't a lie.

Kirkie Algood had been escorted to the station for questions concerning the death of her lover; Poetra Pioll threw herself atop Cana's body and rode with it to the morgue.

A woman in a skimpy white sacrificial costume vaulted a couch and raced into the night, chased by assorted nationalities and the kid with the zoom lens.

"Incredible," Janice said with a shake of her head.

"It has been that," Kent agreed.

"No, I mean, someone stole my clothes."

He raised an eyebrow.

She grinned. "Too right, m'lord. I'm still naked under this itchy thing."

Hazel poked her head out of the cloakroom and asked Janice to let the Inspector know she'd be in, first thing in the morning. Olifer groaned. The door closed. Firmly.

"He was amazing, you know," Kent said as Flora and Eddie waltzed by, trying to drum up business for the pub. "Imagine a songwriter coming up with a scientific breakthrough like that." He sighed. "Just goes to show you what you can do when your back's to the wall."

"He was nuts, Kent."

"Yes. But he was a genius."

"He killed people. Murdered them."

"But his songs will live forever."

Colonel Lumet Braithe (Ret.) staggered by with the cashier in his arms. His monocle protruded between her lips.

"I should thank you for calling the police," Janice called as he staggered toward the elevator.

The colonel leaned against the door and pressed the Up button. "Wasn't my idea." He nodded at the prone but moaning Petula. "My choice was to let you all rot." The door opened. The colonel and the cashier toppled in. "Damn." The door slid shut.

"Naked," Janice said.

Kent said nothing, suddenly aware that he still didn't have a job.

Angus and Lizzy stopped by, arm in arm, faces flushed, eyes glowing, he with a mug in his hand, she wearing his seaman's cap. He blushed, she giggled, and they announced their nuptials within a fortnight.

"Brave man, Angus," Kent said with a laugh.

"Not to worry, sir," he said. "She has me well in hand."

At that, Lizzy snapped her fingers from his coat pocket, boxed him one, and dragged him outside to join a Druid conga-line heading up the High Street.

A minute passed.

Another.

"Well," Janice said.

"Indeed," he answered, and slipped off the counter, stretched as best his injuries would allow. "A hell of a night."

"You wanna lick my nose?"

"You're drunk again," he accused.

"Off duty," she revealed.

He smiled, leaned forward, and froze.

Janice opened her eyes and said, "What? What?"

He pointed.

She looked over her shoulder, through the window, and saw a bearded man in a battered grey western hat, denim jacket, jeans, and black boots ride up onto the sidewalk on a spiffy red motor scooter.

"Kent, who . . . ?"

But Kent was holding his breath.

The man reached into his saddlebag, pulled out a package, and walked into the lobby. After a moment's confusion, he spotted the baron and strode over.

Kent nodded.

The man touched his hat and handed him the package.

"My next script, eh?"

"You got it."

Kent looked at Janice. "Do I have to leave soon?"

The messenger shrugged and left.

"C'mon," Kent said. "Let's walk a little."

She nodded sadly and slipped her hand into his, which made it difficult but not impossible for him to slit open the package and take a peek at the first page.

"I'll be damned."

The air was cool; they turned to the right.

"What?"

"Louisiana," he said. "I've got to go to Louisiana, for god's sake."

"Oh."

He slipped his arm around her waist.

They passed the grocery where Etta Numm counted the grapefruits. She glared. A bulldog in the doorway slobbered and growled. Unless it was Ethel.

"I am," Kent said as they approached Rains Lane, "going to take a room at the Hump. The Bowlingham is too damn noisy tonight." He looked down at the constable. "I don't suppose you have to make a report about your activities."

She shook her head.

She nodded.

She said, "My god!"

"Forget the shaving cream, damnit."

"No! The notebooks!"

He laughed and guided her into the dark alley. "Not to worry, Constable Plase. They're safe and soggy at the bottom of the River George."

She gasped.

"Well, what else could I do? Share his formula with the world? Start a new arms race of a sort? Create havoc and terror among the peoples of the world because they won't know where their next enemy is coming from? Crumple the seats of power? Destroy all that we've created simply because—"

"Okay, okay," she said. Then, a few paces later: "It just seems a shame, that's all. After all those poor people died, it comes out for nothing."

"Oh, I don't know about that," he said. "You did forget your clothes, remember."

They entered the King's Hump, where Zero held court from behind the bar, a silver harmonica strapped around his neck.

"Zero!" Kent called.

The blind man waved back.

"Keep an eye on things, will you? I'm retiring upstairs."

"Stay away from the lab, m'lord," Zuller admonished. "I've got some things cooking."

Kent paused, and thought about his mother.

"Naked," Janice reminded him.

As he leaned over the bar to grab a bottle of Glenbannock, he thought about the remote possibility that some fisherman might accidentally discover the notebooks while trolling upriver, and those same notebooks might not, miraculously, have been destroyed by their submersion.

"Very naked."

As he twisted off the top, he thought about having to do this all again.

Then he took a swig and laughed, saluted Zero, and said, "Here's looking at you, pal."

"Very funny," Zero said.

And Police Constable Janice Plase whipped off her Druid robe, threw his package across the room, and screamed, "Jesus H. Christ, Montana, ain't this over yet?"

THE CREDITS

STARRING AS THEMSELVES:

Kirkie Algood
PC Hazel Bloodlowe
Col. Lumet Braithe (Ret)
Claudius Cana
Racig Dargren
Angus Dean
Insp. Herman Easewater
Dora Feathers
Ralph Geeter
Lizzy Howgath
Eddie Jones
Kent Montana
Etta Numm

Reg Olifer
Poetra Pioll
PC Janice Plase
Ethel Queen
Mary Shweet
Deric Sumland
Flora Tatterall
Petula Vanwort
Gretchen Wain
Stanley Yarkshore
Milo Yonker
Zero Zuller

SPECIAL APPEARANCES BY:

Dove......................................Jerico Dove
Bill the horse............................Bill the elephant
Script Messenger ....Mysterious Person

And:

ARCHIE THE DISGUSTING BULLDOG

Producer .... Northgate 386/20 (a free plug that
didn't work the first time either)
Director...Lionel Fenn
Writer...Lionel Fenn
Editor...................................... Ginjer Buchanan
Music Composed and Arranged by....The Newton Balladeer
Words by .... WordPerfect 5.1
(these free plugs
aren't worth a
damn, you
know)

```
Grip ................................................ ＼ Headlock
Dolly grip⁕......................................... Mr. Parton
Tailor ...............................................Elizabeth
Invisibility Effects.............................
Sergeant Major Costumes...................... Brian Lumley
Druid Costumes ...............................My mother
Legal Advisor....................................... DEW
Pub Advisor...................................Stephen Jones
Location scout ...................................... Tonto
Nudity ......................................... Gratuitous
Sex ............................................ Not tonight
Makeup ......................................Arnold Stang
```

AND SPECIAL THANKS TO:

EmmyLou Harris, Sweethearts of the Rodeo, Willie Nelson, and Reba McEntyre, for C&W inspiration; the Kent Montana Fan Club; and the Merkleton Red Moon Festival, without whom we wouldn't have had any Druids, even if it doesn't exist, which if it doesn't, it ought to.